HOMICIDE CITY 2

Mo' Money, Mo' Homicide

A Novel By

T. Real

Made Man Inc.

ISBN #: 978-0-996270922
Editing and typesetting: Vanna B.
(HopeStreetPublishing.com)
Cover design: Tammy Capri (NuClassPub.com)
Cover model: @missmarinicole

Acknowledgements

First and foremost I thank my creator (He who has many names.) In anything I do from waking up I acknowledge you first. Thank you again for answering my prayers and blessing me and keeping strong through my journey in life. June 29, 2013 you gave me the vision and courage to step out on my own. You let me know how far you brought me, and everything I've seen, lived, and was taught made me into the man I am. And that's why I named my company Made Man.

Thank you to my family, friends, and fans. It's been a long four years I know. Shout out to everyone who bugged me at my job and on Facebook to get this book done. I'm not gonna lie; this was a rough patch for me but I got through. I wanted this to be as special as the first time I held the book when it was first released. I promise more books are on the way. I got a few more surprises on the way. #MadeMan

Shout out to my model on the front cover, Miss Mari Nicole. You did an awesome job. Of course you got on my nerves about this cover but it's cool. Shout out to Tammy Capri over at Nu Class Publications for the hot covers. Can't wait to see what we cook up for the part three cover. And lastly, Vanna B. from Hope Street Publishing, thanks for the great editing job.

Now if you're reading this right now I thank you for taking your time to read. I welcome you all to *Homicide City 2: Mo' Money Mo' Homicide.*

Enjoy, Author T. Real, Owner of Made Man Inc.

<u>Dedications</u>

I dedicate this book to Marquis "Abdus Shakur" Battle. April 9th 2013 still seems unreal but it's a reality. And to anyone who lost a family member to senseless violence, I dedicate this book to you all.

Introduction

Screech, screech! The plane tires sounded as they hit the landing strip of LAX jerking Erica from her slumber. She yawned, blinked five times, and then stretched to fully awaken. Glancing at her watch she knew she had the wrong time because it didn't match up with how bright and sunny it was.

The City of Angels, she thought to herself.

Gathering her thoughts before the flight attendant came over the intercom to go over the instructions on exiting the plane, Erica leaned over and whispered to the male passenger seated next to her.

"Excuse me sir. How do you determine the time on the West Coast?"

"You roll your time back four hours."

Erica smiled and thanked the man for the lesson in time zones as the attendant came over the loud speaker explaining the exit routine and seat belts. One principle Erica learned from her father that she always abided by in public was patience. Never move in haste because haste is waste and always look attentive because someone is always watching. His wisdom replayed in her mind, as she knew once the plane came to a complete stop and people were ready to evacuate the shoving match was going to begin. As she expected, she sat back and watched as passengers began to grab their luggage from the overhead compartments, bumping each other. Erica shook her head and chuckled at the slight melee. One flight attendant noticed she was sitting still maneuvered through the line to come check on her.

"Are you okay Miss?" she asked.

"Yes I'm okay. I'm not in a rush to get bumped. I'm waiting until it clears a little. Then I will grab my belongings and exit."

The flight attendant just smirked and nodded then walked away.

"Nosey bitch," Erica mumbled under her breath as she stood up and grabbed her Dooney and Bourke purse out of the compartment above her.

After retrieving her bag she pulled out her cell phone turned it on and began to exit the plane by walking into the jet bridge. After exiting the terminal she let out a sigh at the sight of all the travelers then she began to read the signs for baggage claim. She glanced at her cell phone to see if she had any bars to make a call. With two being available she was able to dial Mr. Hard. She chuckled to herself at the fact that she had the man stored under that name, and after three rings he answered.

"I'm just about to pull up. What flight were you on?"

"AirTran, but look, my stomach is talking to me," Erica said while her stomach let out a few groans.

"Well what are you in the mood for?" Mr. Hard responded after laughing at the mention of her hunger pains.

Erica stopped in her tracks then remembered the info she looked at while browsing online.

"Two places; Fat Burger and Roscoe's Chicken and Waffles."

"Cool, we will figure out one to go to."

"Okay, I'm hanging up. See you after I grab my luggage from baggage claim."

They both hung up as Erica proceeded to retrieve her luggage. Once she reached her destination she managed to squirm her way in the middle of two men dressed in suits. With her eyes focused on the machine going in a circle to see if her bags arrived she didn't notice both of the men admiring every curve on her body. The feeling of four eyes beaming caught her attention as she perused to her left then right of her observers.

"May I help you?" Erica asked as she spotted one of her suitcases then walked over to grab it.

The man to her left answered, taking off his Louis Vuitton shades. Erica noticed how dapper both men were and wondered what their occupations were. After making her observation, the man to her left went inside his left pocket and pulled out a business card then began speaking.

"Hello, my name is Mark Graham, and to ya right is my brother Rico. We are the CEOs of Star Power Entertainment."

Now that his sunglasses were off his face Erica noticed the resemblance.

"Thank you for the card," Erica said.

"No, thank you for taking it. I mean excuse us for looking like pedophiles when you stepped between us but you're gorgeous. What are you, a movie star?"

Erica blushed at his questioning.

"No, why do you ask?"

"Only a movie star could have a man holding a sign up with their name on it."

Erica's face scrunched up in confusion as she began to look around to see what he was talking about.

"No, no, over there." Mark pointed over to where a 6'3" dark-skinned man was holding a sign up displaying her government name.

Erica smiled at the gesture of Mr. Hard, and was curious at the same time of how Mark knew it was her.

"How did you know it was for me?"

Mark pointed down to her suitcase as her tag displayed her first and last name.

"Look, I'm very observant and I can spot a star from a mile away so please give us a call when you're ready."

Erica spotted her last piece of luggage. Her anxiety was high but not to the point that she was shaking profusely. It was because she was happy. The actions of Mr. Hard had her on cloud nine, plus she was being scouted in public.

"Thank you Mr. Graham. When I get time I will give you guys a call," Erica said while walking away towards the man holding the sign with her name on it.

"Hello, I'm Erica Williams."

"Pleased to meet you. I'm your assistant Amaziah."

"Amaziah. That sounds like a name with a great meaning," Erica said, complementing the man.

"Yes it's Hebrew for strength of God."

Erica was a little confused since the man was dark like an African, but she didn't take the conversation any further. After the brief introduction Amaziah grabbed her belongings then lead the way outside. Erica grunted and complimented the dark handsome man.

"Yes, and your parents named you correctly," Erica said at the sight of him man handling the luggage with no apparent strain.

Amaziah led her to a black on black Range Rover stretch limo. The door opened and Mr. Hard hopped out matching the vehicle from head to toe. He and Erica embraced briefly.

"What's up with the all black? Did you attend a funeral today?"

Mr. Hard chuckled at her question before answering.

"No time for questions. Just hop in and I will explain everything."

Erica was wowed by how plush the interior was as she spotted the crystal wet bar. When she sat down she felt as if she was sinking. The first thing she noticed though was the three females who were dressed in all black skirts occupying the seats in front of her. She decided to wait until she was introduced to them to speak. Erica was never the one to be intimidated by another female but she knew by the looks of them they were of high importance. After the brief admiration of the vehicle and passengers Mr. Hard interrupted.

"So what's up Erica?"

Erica turned and looked Mr. Hard directly in his eyes.

"Nothing much. You tell me."

"Let's talk over a glass of chardonnay. Kimmie could you pour us both a glass please?"

Kimmie, one of the three passengers who looked to be Hawaiian, reached over to the wet bar, poured them both glasses, and passed one to each of them. Erica took a sip from her glass then the conversation picked up where it left off.

"This wine is going to burn a hole through my stomach. I don't think I should be drinking on an empty stomach."

"You gon' be straight. It's only one glass. Plus we on our way to Roscoe's. Then after that we taking you to purchase an all-black outfit of your choice so you can hang with us tonight," Mr. Hard stated.

"Oh okay, that's what's up," Erica said with excitement written on her face. "So what you out here pimping nigga?" Erica asked right after.

Mr. Hard laughed wholeheartedly at her slight interrogation, almost spilling his wine. He took another sip, swallowed, then answered.

"No I run a webcam enterprise and these three are my MVPs that bring me the benjis. You already know Kimmie, that's Corinne, my Brazilian beauty, and last that's Salene. She's from London. What would make this complete is some chocolate fresh from Philly.

As he was done Mr. Hard pulled out his business card and passed it to Erica.

"Damn, what, everybody pulls out a business card on you in L.A?" Erica said jokingly.

Mr. Hard chuckled himself before commenting.

"Girl you crazy but this ain't Philly where you recruit with words. You got to show some type of authenticity from the jump."

"I mean just 'cause you got a card don't mean you not frauding Terrence."

Mr. Hard chuckled once again at the fact she called him by his government name after seeing it on his card.

"So what's it gon' be? I didn't fly you out here to bullshit you around. I want you to join my empire."

Erica stared at the card then glanced at the three international beauties.

"I will have my answer by the end of the night."

$$$$

Bishop Williams sat in his study as he was indulging in one of his routines, reading the daily newspaper before his appointments began. While perusing to see how the city was shaping itself, he came across an article titled "Deadly Weekend: Five Dead." He shook his head as he began to read about the senseless murders across the city. One important detail he noticed in the article was that the people who lost their lives were between the ages of 18-25.

"They haven't even begun to experience the joys of life," Bishop spoke out loud, expressing his concern at what he just read. "It seems we are falling back into being statistics," he stated before he dropped his head and began to pray for the fallen. "Father I know you always hear me. Please lend me the power, the strength, the will to stop these senseless murders. I beg unto you, use me in any way need be Father, to guide and to protect. Even though it's a part of life I will continue to pray for our communities and for the destruction of the weak and merciless over money, power, and respect. And thank you, for what I pray for the world I pray for my own family. Please protect us and whatever lessons we need to learn from our own actions let them be lessons learned and let us walk away unscathed and stronger. Amen."

Bishop Williams raised his head, exhaled, then walked over to his desk to look over his itinerary for the day. He had to make sure none of them ran into the time he needed to pick up DJ from school. Once he was done glancing over his schedule he walked over to his closet and put on his robe he wore during meetings, preparing for his first appointment. Knowing he had ten minutes left to spare he went into his desk and pulled out his Blackberry. He noticed he had two missed calls from Erica and a text message. He read the message that stated she arrived and she would call back. He was about to call back but his first appointment walked in and interrupted that process. Bishop Williams glared at the person, waiting for an explanation of why they were standing in his office. He shook his head as he looked at the name on the sheet, as it didn't match up with the face.

"Well long time no see Bishop. I know I'm a sight for sore eyes," the lady said. She sported a black fitted Carolina Herrera dress with the heels to match.

"Yes Vanity Jackson. How long has it been?" Bishop asked as he stared at how the dress complimented her thickness and brown skin tone. After admiring her thighs and curves his eyes wandered up to her face as her clear Mac lipstick accentuated the shape of her plump lips. Bishop was mesmerized by the beauty he hadn't seen in years.

"To answer your question it's been five years, but who's counting? You stare at me like we never lost a step."

"So what brings you in my neck of the woods?"

Still standing in front of Bishop Vanity responded back.

"Bishop I have come to thank you in person since you've been ignoring my calls."

"Well under the circumstances of life I've moved on."

"Is that so? Well we will see about that," Vanity said while showing off her pearly whites.

Bishop didn't want to dignify her statement so he ignored her and remained silent and emotionless. But yet and still the sight of Vanity made his temperature rise.

"Oh and where are my manners? You may have a seat." Bishop gestured towards the seat in front of her.

"Thank you I was waiting for you let me know when I could sit," Vanity said in a sassy way before sitting down and getting down to business.

"Let me get straight to the point of why I'm here Bishop. From having meetings with you in the past I was able to get on my feet and start a non-profit."

"Well congratulations to you on having large aspirations and being an inspiration."

Vanity beamed as she continued.

"Yes thanks to you. I was inspired by your words to change and now I change the lives of women at risk to go down the same path I was once on."

Her words brought a smile to Bishop's face as he thought she was only here to be the bearer of bad news.

"Now with your blessings and your financial backing I can make my non-profit even bigger, starting with my biggest challenge."

Once Vanity was done speaking she reached into her bag and dropped a DVD on top of his desk. Bishop picked up the DVD and noticed Erica on the cover holding a penis to her mouth with the title "Head Doctors" above her head.

"What is this? Some sick joke?" Bishop asked while slinging the DVD back in her direction.

"No, but I'm smart enough to know you knew about this. Plus she's in need of help and heading down the same road I once was on so why not start with her?"

Bishop took a deep breath and remained silent as he thought about what she was saying.

"I mean I don't see any harm Vanity with you stepping in. She might be able to use some words of wisdom from somebody that's familiar with that lifestyle. I'm sorry for the way I reacted at first."

"It's okay Bishop. I accept your apology. Now how fast can you facilitate a meeting between the two of us?"

"She's out in California taking a vacation so I don't see it happening any time soon. Let me contact her first then I will let you know."

Vanity dug in her purse then stood up.

"Okay well here's my card and when you speak to her don't forget to call me."

Bishop ignored her for a brief second while he admired the business card she handed him.

"Very Impressive. I sure won't forget. So now I guess this meeting is over."

"Far from over," she replied as she walked around the desk pushed the chair away from the desk.

"Now that we got Erica out of the way, it's time to help daddy out," Vanity said seductively.

She reached for his zipper to begin seducing him but was unsuccessful. Bishop was saved by a knock on his door from his second meeting of the day.

$$$$

Captain Morello sat in front of his computer clicking through the prompts to erasing the files for his falling Sgt. He came up on the last one that read "Delete or cancel." He clicked delete and the file for Frank Moretti was deleted. He took a deep breath. He couldn't believe what had taken place in his department, which from the incident was under the scope by City Hall and Internal Affairs. It was just a matter of time before the suits started to arrive and begin their own investigation and interrogating the precinct. As he arose from his chair to get some coffee a knock came at his door.

"You may enter," Captain Morello stated.

Officer Freeman entered his captain's office with his uniform sharp as a tack.

"Looking good Freeman," Captain Morello said, taking pride in his officer's appearance.

"Thank you Captain. I wanted to make sure I made a good impression since you called me in."

"Good choice. Now that you're here let's get this meeting underway," Captain Morello said while extending his arm in the direction of the chair in front of his desk.

Officer Freeman sat down after receiving the permission to sit as the meeting began.

A short silence fell upon the men as Captain Morello searched for the correct words to start the meeting. After a brief stare down the Captain began to speak.

"So Freeman do you have any idea why I called this meeting between us?"

Officer Freeman unloosened his collar and chuckled before answering.

"To tell you the truth sir that brief silence made me a little nervous. I have all types of reasons swirling through my brain."

Captain Morello chuckled at his officer's nervousness.

"No need to be nervous. This is a mere meeting, not an interrogation. First and foremost I'm letting you know since the passing of your fellow Sgt. you will be rising in the ranks of this precinct and presiding."

"Thank you sir," Officer Freeman said through a small grin.

Captain Morello raised his hand to signal he was not finished.

"Second I just want to ask you a few questions before you officially receive your stripes and I make the announcement. Now how well did you know your Sgt. before the incident happened?"

Officer Freeman exhaled then answered.

"Sir all I know is we were on the trail of a rap entourage connecting them to what was transpiring in the streets with the Jamaicans. Anything outside of that I'm clueless."

"Okay Freeman I just wanted to know if you knew anything extra because as you should know anytime an officer dies IA comes crawling to start their own investigation."

"I'm aware of that Captain. And what I just explained will be same thing I tell them. Now not to change the subject but how are you taking it sir?"

Captain Morello arose from his chair then stared out his office window as he spoke.

"I'm okay despite losing a good officer and I don't care what rumors are floating around or who accused him of what. He was a damn good officer and that's how he rose in the ranks. I don't know where he took a wrong turn but I will find out once IA arrives. And let me tell you once they arrive things will never be the same around here."

Officer Freeman's face balled up in confusion.

"Accusations, rumors, sir I'm confused. I never—"

Captain Morello raised his hand again to stop his newly appointed Sgt. from speaking as two men dressed in suits with fresh creases in their pants and black shoes shined to perfection walked into his office without warning.

"Captain Morello good to see you again. You know me, Officer Davis and my partner, Officer Jennings from IA.

"Certainly, I've been awaiting your arrival," Captain Morello stated.

"Great, we are here to began conducting our investigation," Officer Davis stated as Officer Jennings closed the door.

$$$$

Tony Moretti stood outside the late Johnny Capers' house along with his henchmen Paulie and Severino. Following the orders Tony spat, Severino knocked on the front door. A 150-pound beauty appeared, peeking through the front window to see the culprits knocking and arriving unexpectedly. Disarming the ADT system Sophie opened the front door.

"Tony come on in," Sophie said while walking towards the living room area.

During her short trip back to the plush leather couch Severino gazed at her ass as it bounced up and down inside her black sheer tights.

"Too bad Johnny's not here to enjoy that anymore."

Tony and Paulie chuckled at Severino's perversion.

"Yeah I always complimented him on his taste in women. God bless the dead," Tony commented.

Sophie sat down then paused her favorite show Mob Wives, as Paulie pulled a chair from the dining room table and placed it in the same area. After attending to his boss Severino stood on his left as Paulie stood over his right shoulder.

"So what's been up Sophie? How are you feeling?"

Sophie let out a hard sigh then spoke. Her voice instantly cracked as she sobbed about Johnny.

"Tony you know I loved Johnny to death. I miss him so much," Sophie sniffled while displaying her emotional state for her late fiancé.

She held out her hand and displayed the diamond her bought her before his untimely demise.

"He proposed a week before his death and now all I do is watch Mob Wives reruns and look at my favorite picture of us."

After she spoke she reached over on the black marble table in front of her and picked up a framed photo and displayed to Moretti a picture of her and Johnny one night at the Borgata in Atlantic City.

Tony passed it to Severino and Paulie for them to see and then Tony placed it back on the table.

"How touching," Severino stated, making Paulie snicker.

Tony raised his hand to dismiss any wisecracks due to the severity of why he was in her presence.

"Listen Sophie, Johnny and Joey are not here due to being disloyal to the family. They tried to make moves outside my guidelines and got clipped. To be even more sincere on why I'm here, I'm collecting his debts so any money he saved up, and that diamond ring, give it up."

"But Tony—"

Tony raised his hand, cutting off any more pleas that were sure to come.

"Let me make myself crystal clear. I'm not asking. I'm telling you."

Sophie sprung up like a jack in the box, running upstairs then returning with Benjamins wrapped in 5K bank stickers covered. Placing them in Tony's hand she sat back in the same spot on the couch like a trained puppy.

"Very good Sophie," Tony verbalized while passing the stacks to Paulie.

Paulie placed them on the right inside pocket of his suit then dropped his arms back to his waist side.

"Now the ring," Tony demanded, extending his right arm.

Sophie's eyes welled up with tears as she stared at Tony while grasping the ring and holding it close to her heart.

"Tony don't take it away. Please, this is the last thing he bought me that I hold on to dearly."

Tony sighed at the sight of Sophie's tears but his heart was colder than Alaska. He didn't feel an ounce of remorse since he was the one that pulled the trigger taking Johnny's life for his disloyal behavior, so he knew a diamond wouldn't warm his heart up. He glanced up over his left shoulder at Severino and spoke.

"Severino convince her to take the ring off. I don't have time for negotiations."

Severino followed the command of his boss and walked over to Sophie, entering her space. She budged, trying to make a move away from his grasp but was unsuccessful as he grabbed her ponytail. He then reached into his lower back area, pulling out a nickel-plated .32 and placing it under her chin.

"Listen, you got five seconds to take the ring off, starting now."

Sophie almost ripped her skin off by snatching the ring off.

"Good, now that we got his debts out of the way, let me know how are you making ends meet now that he's six feet under?"

"I was living off of the money Tony," Sophie said as she wept.

"Well you're in luck. I need someone to manage my bar and you're the perfect candidate. You're smart and pretty. You could make a lot of money. Oh, before I leave I need a favor. Your best friends with Joey Capers' girl, right?"

"Yeah Tony, what about her?" Sophie asked, instantly becoming paranoid.

Tony stood up, dusting off his suit then answered.

"Oh nothing, just give her a courtesy call and tell her we are on our way to collect."

Tony pulled out a crisp Benjamin and placed it on the marble table.

"That's for ya troubles and wipe those tears away. Crying over spilled milk is so overrated."

$$$$

Maria stood over her sink with the water running, completing the last wash and rinse of the plates and cups her and Michelle used for dinner. After placing them to her right inside the dish rack, she began wiping down the excess water and emptying the sink of dishwater.

Knock, knock! The door to the backyard shed caught her attention as the night wind blew it open.

Maria placed the dishrag on the sink and walked over to the sliding door that led to the backyard. She didn't want to investigate but she also didn't want the noise to wake up Michelle who was put to sleep an hour ago. The thought of how it was opened crossed her mind as she turned on the backyard light, coming to the conclusion she forgot to put the lock on earlier. As soon as she stepped outside she folded her arms across her chest as the slight breeze blew right through her shirt causing goose bumps to form. The door flew open as she tiptoed over, causing her to become startled quickly and she ran over to try to hurry up and lock it. She was almost successful until she was gripped by the wrist and pulled inside the shed. Before she could let out a scream a hand came across her mouth, muzzling her. Maria's breathing became heavier and heavier in the tight clutch as she was clueless to what was about to take place. The culprit who snatched her in the shed began to speak.

"Babe whatever you do don't panic. It's me," the man said as he let her go and turned on the light.

Even after recognizing the voice and face Maria tried to beat the man to a bloody pulp after being released.

"It can't be. I buried you! I buried you Frank! Maria yelled as she landed a couple of combos to his chest.

Frank tried to dodge the sparring match but failed as the punches landed successfully. He ended the melee by grabbing her arms.

"Look, I know it's a lot to take in at the moment but calm down," Frank said, looking Maria directly in her eyes.

Maria agreed to stop as she wiped her face of the tears that flowed.

"Now that we got that out of the way are you ready for what I got to tell you?"

Maria took a deep breath then nodded to her husband.

"Okay, the car explosion I know that was a little over the edge but it was—"

Maria caught him in mid sentence.

"A hoax! Do you know what you put me and your daughter through? How many nights I laid crying myself to sleep from that whole ordeal? Do you? Do you?! Maria yelled.

If the door was open she would have awakened Michelle and a couple of neighbors.

"Maria I know it was painful to even witness or live through the whole ordeal but—"

"But nothing you motherfucker. I should bury you right now myself," Maria said while perusing the shed without moving.

"What the hell are you looking for?" Frank asked, following her eye movement.

"An axe and a shovel," Maria answered.

Frank chuckled at the notion that his wife wasn't joking. She was just as crazy as he was and that was the reason why they were married.

"Maria I missed you. Is that what you want to hear? I love you and I missed you," Frank said while pulling her closely for a tight hug and kissing her forehead.

"And what about your daughter, huh? Maria asked as her words vibrated his chest.

"I love her and missed her too. Now can we take this reunion inside? "

"So if you loved us so much why did you do what you did? What was so bad about being a cop?

"Let's go inside and I will tell you," Frank said, getting impatient.

Maria removed herself from the clutches of her husband and turned to walk out the shed but hesitated.

"No, we can stay in here for our conversation. I don't even know how Michelle is going to take the news of her father being buried then seeing him. How are you going to explain that one genius?"

Frank did his usual chuckle then answered.

"Believe me, I have it all mapped out."

$$$$

The bass line from the Ying Yang Twins' "Saltshaker" could be heard coming through Benji's office walls as he shimmied his shoulders left and right, counting money at the same time. He even sang to the lyrics as the bills slipped through his fingertips.

"She leakin', she soaking wet, she leakin', she soaking wet. Shake it like a saltshaker, shake it like a saltshaker."

After his brief two minutes of singing along he counted his last twenty-dollar bill and put them all neatly into a stack. He then opened his money drawer, placing the countings inside then sat down and kicked his feet up.

"The life of a boss. Three more dancers and my count is done for the night," Benji said aloud.

Seconds later a couple of knocks interrupted his comfort as Benji yelled out to the visitor that they could enter. Entering was Mocha and when she walked inside his office Benji smiled at the fact that she was bringing him his money. Mocha swung the door behind her as she walked in to pay but before the door closed Omar caught the door and caught her while she was in stride with a nice smack on her ass. To his dismay Benji corrected his actions.

"Hey Omar, treat my girls with respect," Benji said as he walked around his desk and hugged Mocha.

Omar flagged Benji before sitting down and watching Mocha and Benji interact.

"And you're gracing my presence because?" Benji asked Mocha like he didn't know why she was standing in front of him.

"Don't play stupid Benji. You know its payday," Mocha answered while reaching into the left breast side of her bikini top, pulling out a wad of dead presidents.

Benji grinned like the cat on the Cheetos bag at the sight of the greenbacks he was about to receive.

"Is that all for me?" he asked while rubbing his hands together.

"Man just take the damn money. I got something to pass down to you," Omar interrupted from the sideline.

Both Mocha and Benji scrunched their faces up looking in the direction of Omar.

"I'm sorry for the interruption but we will talk later," Benji said while placing the money in his pocket then wrapping his arm around her waist to escort her out properly. As soon as she was out the door he turned around to school Omar.

"Omar my man, two things you need to know right now. Never interrupt a money transaction. Second, you have to respect the girls at all costs."

"C'mon Benji, you don't have to school me to any game. It's not like I'm new around here."

Benji took a deep breath before responding.

"Everything I've been teaching you has been going in one ear and out the other. Listen, everything I tell you is to put you in position. At the moment your just head of my security but if you play ya cards right you can own this as soon as the main spot opens back up. Now I'm hoping when that happens you can run this spot as smoothly as I do."

Omar shook his head before answering.

"I respect ya words but you don't have faith in me."

"It's not that. Well let me ask you this. How are you going to run this business successfully? You don't see me smacking asses. If you want them to respect you then you have to respect them. Especially if they are handing you money 'cause let me tell you, the first time I disrespect one it spreads like the plague then all hell breaks loose. Every ass that walks through that door is gon' think they can short me cause I like smacking asses."

Omar nodded in agreement at Benji's Strip Club 101.

"You know what, you're right Benji, but a lesson in respecting these hos is not what I came in here for."

"Well what is it? Benji asked.

"Word on the street is a couple of ya girls is already disrespecting you by selling ass out of here."

Benji glared at Omar as the words began to process through his ears to his brain. Out of all the years he owned strip clubs he warned he girls never to sell ass in his establishments.

"Being head of my security did you investigate to see who that might be?"

"No. But with all that heat from that shootout it's not needed."

"You know what, you're right Omar. I mean who knows if my business here is not being watched from that incident. God forbid it's true then this club gets shut down too."

After speaking Benji sighed then stood up then began to walk back and forth nervously. Omar turned his head slightly to the left while observing his boss.

"Hey Benji you okay? It's not that deep man. I'm here to give you the heads up. But just know I'm on it like flies on shit man."

"I'm good Omar. Just thinking about the cops now. You know the thought of cops makes me nervous. Speaking of cops though have you seen them lately?"

"Not since the last time they came when you were here."

"Good, good. The focus is on making that transition back to the old spot and making you into a boss. I'm not the one for rumors but if what you told me is true what's done in the dark shall come to the light," Benji said before another knock came across his door.

"You can enter!" Benji yelled then peeked at his list.

"That's either Sexi Lexi or Poison. They are always the last to pay," Benji said, anticipating his last payments.

"Not to rain on ya parade boss man but that sounded like a cop knock," Omar stated.

After Omar spoke one of Benji's burly security guys, Reg, stepped in with two Caucasian men in suits.

"Benji these two men would like to speak to you," Reg stated as he closed the door as he walked out.

"How can I help you two gentlemen?" Benji asked, being cordial and standing up to greet them. Omar was silent on the sideline as he stared at the two men.

"Yes I'm Agent Daniels and this is my partner Agent Corley. We are here to speak to Mr. Anthony Freeman."

"I'm Anthony Freeman," Benji chuckled nervously as he extended his hand out for a handshake like a true businessman.

The agents were in attendance for business but handshakes weren't given out.

Agent Daniels pulled out a large brown envelope and emptied the contents on Benji's desk.

"Please feel free to glance through these photos. They are photos of the night of the shootout at your club," Agent Daniels said, getting the attention of both Benji and Omar as they both began to skim through the photos.

As they both looked, slowly passing the photos between each other Agent Corley spoke up.

"Sir just to let you know we are taking the case from the locals since this case is going federal. We need to know detail after detail of what took place the night of the shootout."

$$$$

While the streetlights shined bright over the concrete jungle the whole Gwap Gang was in attendance at Chance's wall memorial. Having what they called a meeting was more like their fifth memorial for Chance. Meet ups were the norm here since Chance was murdered as they felt like when they met there Chance was there in spirit. Dutches filled with the finest marijuana and Ciroc bottles were being passed around. The air was thick in the midst of the sips and puffs that were being taken. The only words that were spoken at first was when everybody paid their respects by pouring out a li'l liquor for their homie. Banks was the last to pour out on the curb then he spoke to his entourage.

"I don't know if I'm speaking for myself about being in the dark, but what's next for us?"

Everybody was silent as they took in the words from Banks, while looking around for someone to answer and break the silence. Chase Money hesitated due to taking a couple of puffs from the Dutch but after he exhaled he spoke up.

"To tell you the truth bro I don't know. I mean we done went to war and my bro is six feet. I say we focus on getting back on track."

After speaking Chase Money looked around to see what type of response he received only for Banks to respond back.

"You right Chase. I mean what we got to lose? Our name and bread is on the line right now as we speak. But to keep it 100 with all y'all I'm not willing to lose my position over no more bullshit."

Everybody shook hands in agreement with Banks as his words brought a positive spark. But only Chase Money and Banks conversed.

"I feel you Banks. From what transpired we got to be even smarter now when we move through these streets. We got enemies, plus we got to remain on top of our paper."

"Man fuck enemies. I got a hot one for each and every one of them," Paperboi said while pulling out his Glock 19 and cocking it.

Everyone chuckled at his actions as Chase continued.

"Listen as bad as I wanna say fuck money and get at them niggas who shot my brother that would go against our true agenda. With that being said give everything time to make them think we letting it ride and when the time is right all them niggas is D.O.A."

$$$$

Amani staggered out of Kif's Sports Bar and Lounge to get some air and to smoke a bidi. Dapper with his green, black, and yellow Jamaican sports jacket, black jeans, and Nike Air Runners to match his jacket, his dreads flowed straight back in a ponytail. Heavily intoxicated from taking shots of Henny and drinking numerous bottles of Guinness, he searched for his lighter, tapping his jacket and jean pockets. After locating his lighter he sparked his bidi and leaned up against the wall. While taking a deep pull he slipped, losing his balance and almost met the pavement but regained his balance. Across the street three partygoers who stood inside a Chinese store witnessed the comedy. Amani could hear the laughter coming from the hecklers and stuck his middle finger up in their direction. After regaining his balance and continuing to smoke he spotted a figure coming from around the corner on the block he stood with a black hoodie and dreads coming from up under.

"Brethren, brethren," Amani said, acknowledging his fellow dread in passing.

Before the unknown pedestrian could pass him he asked him for a lighter to spark the cigarette he held in his hand.

"Here you go fam," Amani said while passing him the lighter.

While passing him the lighter Amani didn't notice the culprit pulling out a black weapon with a long nose silencer on the front. Two shots were fired hitting Amani in the abdomen. Amani staggered back to the wall then dropped to his knees. After clutching his wounds he fell on his stomach to take his final breaths. The three women who were in the Chinese store across from Amani grabbed their food and walked out. On their way to their car they spotted Amani lying on the pavement. One spoke on what the two others were laughing at.

"Look at this drunk nigga passed out on the pavement. We should go in his pockets," Keisha stated.

They all looked at each other while standing at the car deciding what move to make.

"C'mon let's do it. He look like he got a couple of dollars on him," Dominique said.

Raquel was the only one that didn't budge. She just watched as her two close friends were about to rob him unknowing of what just took place.

"Look, what if he wakes up and smacks the shit out of you both?" Raquel said while they both walked over.

"Bitch he's passed out. He ain't waking up no time soon," Keisha responded while kneeling down to roll him over. The first sight of the blood that leaked from his gunshot wounds made her scream at the top of her lungs.

$$$$

With her legs spread apart and Omar splashing inside the puddle between her thighs Detective

Richmond's hands gripped her headboard. With every stroke received from Omar her moans and the knocks on the wall came in unison. With his hands positioned on both her breasts Omar watched with enjoyment the sex faces Natasha was showcasing. As the feeling of a climax was arising he switched speeds, which made her moan even louder. Omar released his grip on her breasts and fell on top of her as they lay chest to chest breathing heavily in each other's ears. Omar then began to kiss her neck gently but was interrupted by the ringing of her cell phone.

"Don't answer it," Omar said in between the pecks on her neck.

"Sorry I have to answer. It's my job phone," Detective Richmond said while reaching for it.

"What's up partner?" she answered.

"We got a 187 between 62nd and 63rd and Market. Meet me at Kif's Sports Bar and Lounge ASAP," Detective Patterson said then hung up.

Detective Richmond quickly jumped up and turned on her lamp and proceeded to her bathroom to freshen up from the sexual romp. Omar watched from the comfort of her bed with the sheets covering him from waist down.

"Duty calls," Omar stated, not wanting her to leave.

"As always. You know how crazy this city is," Detective Richmond answered back from the bathroom while turning on the shower.

After her brief cleansing she came out wrapped in a peach colored towel, walked over to Omar lying in the same position, leaned over top of him, and kissed him on the chest.

"I thank you for the release. I was tense from work."

Omar grinned from ear to ear as her words stroked every inch of his ego. He reached under the towel and palmed her bare wet ass while he spoke.

"You're welcome Ms. Richmond, but I think you need to get up before I make you late."

"You lucky that call saved you or you would be putting in overtime buddy," Detective Richmond responded as she got up to get dressed.

As she went into her closet Omar received a text message. He glanced over the message then arose from the bed.

"Look I know I said I was going to stay but I got some unfinished business to attend to at the club."

Natasha responded back from inside the closet as she was busying herself with getting dressed.

"No problem. I will probably be tied up from what happened tonight anyway. Don't worry, we will catch up to each other," she said as she put on her shoes and grabbed her badge, gun, and holster.

After grabbing her keys she walked over to Omar who was standing in his birthday suit in front of her bathroom. She stood in front of him admiring his sexiness and grabbed his manhood then kissed his chest.

"You don't mind if I use ya shower before I go, do you?" Omar asked while receiving the tender kisses.

"No, not at all. I wouldn't want none of your li'l girlfriends from the club getting jealous from you carrying my scent."

Omar chuckled.

"Naw I don't think nothing like that would happen."

"Good 'cause I don't wanna lose my job for putting a hot on in one of your fans," Detective Richmond said while reaching for her gun.

They both chuckled at her response as they embraced and kissed then Omar watched as Detective Richmond left to handle her business in the streets.

$$$$

Squad cars stretched from 62nd and 63rd and Market like it was a police convention. Red and blue lights lit up the block as the caution tape was wrapped around the scene Amani's body laid. Onlookers from inside the party were spread out in the street. The females were crying in disbelief that he was just inside with them partying and now they were looking at him about to be taken to the morgue. Detective Patterson pulled up in all the chaos and walked up on the scene of the crime where the helicopter shined their light. After looking over the scene and making sure CSI didn't move anything until he collected the proper notes, he began to look around for any potential

33

witness to collect info from and spotted Keisha and her crew. With him being considered a vet he could now spot who was going to give him what he needed and who was going to stay silent.

"Hey ladies, did you know the deceased?" Detective Patterson asked as he walked up on them.

"And who are you?" Keisha asked with attitude deeply rooted in her voice.

"Oh my bad. I forgot to show my badge," Detective Patterson said while he laughed off Keisha's ignorance, reaching in his suit pocket and pulling out his badge and flashing it to them.

"Now that I got that out of the way, did any one of you three ladies know the deceased?"

"No officer we are the ones that found him lying here and ran over to the police car that was posted up by the Motorcycle Club," Keisha answered while Raquel and Dominique stood by silent.

Detective Patterson took out his note pad, jotted down a few notes, then proceeded to his next questions.

"So could you walk me through how you found him. And please try to be as detailed as possible."

"We were inside that Chinese store across the street. We saw him come out of the party to smoke. He was drunk stumbling over the place while doing so and almost fell. We got our food walked over to where our car was parked and we spotted him lying there. We thought he had passed out so we walked over to get him up and that's when we spotted the blood and everything."

"Okay back up a little for me. You spotted him laying here as you walked over from the Chinese store?"

"Yes that's what happened," Keisha answered.

"So you three never heard any gunshots," Detective Patterson asked.

"No sir, that's why we thought he had passed out," Keisha responded.

"Okay makes sense. Thank you ladies for your cooperation."

Detective Patterson made sure he wrote down all the notes before he walked off. He didn't want to miss any details. After gathering that info he went back over to where the shell casings were circled and wrote down how many were found. Once he finished he heard a familiar voice come up from behind.

"What's up partner? Where are we at on the scene," Detective Richmond asked.

"Well, well, look who decided to show up," Detective Patterson said jokingly.

Detective Richmond rolled her eyes at her partner then flagged him.

"Look I was here. I stopped over and was speaking to the pack of dreads that were out here. Of course it was like talking to a brick wall. They didn't give me shit to go off of. But I did spot on the vehicles they were driving. They all had stickers that read "The Posse.""

"Cool. That might come in handy. I interviewed the three girls who notified police and they said they didn't hear any gunshots."

"Hmmm, that's interesting," Detective Richmond responded as they both walked over to where the coroner was waiting to get the word to wrap up the scene.

"You guys are clear," Detective Patterson said as they picked the body up, en route to the morgue.

"Well we might as well be headed to the station to start this paperwork," Detective Patterson said as they separated to walk to their cars. While walking towards his car Detective Patterson was swarmed by reporters who were waiting for a chance to get the scoop on what transpired.

"Detective! Detective! Any info you can give us on what has taken place?" the Channel 3 male news reporter asked.

"At this moment all I can say is there was a homicide tonight and we hope to catch the culprit who committed the crime."

"Thanks now in other news about the 18th District, did you guys ever catch the guy who blew up that Sgt?"

"Now you would have to call into the precinct to find that out," Detective Patterson said as he slammed his door, started his car, then drove off.

$$$$

Back at the precinct both Detectives Patterson and Richmond sat across from each other going back over notes and scenarios. The station was quiet due to the night shift having more cops on patrol then on duty then in the office.

"So what you think partner? Premeditated?" Richmond asked.

Detective Patterson stood up, sipped his coffee, then sat his mug back down before answering.

"I'm thinking he made beef at the party or somebody knew he was going to be there and got the drop on him, *pop, pop*, end of story."

Detective Richmond sat back and replayed his scenario in her head. She nodded then responded back with her own.

"Makes sense but who in their right mind would let somebody get that close that they didn't know?"

"My notes show he wasn't in his right mind. Remember the three females across the street at the Chinese store said he was intoxicated."

"Okay well that proves my point. Premeditated, since they knew he was going to be there at his weakest point, at a party drunk.

Detective Patterson, silent from listening, smiled at how his partner was sly with her detection.

"You know what, that makes even more sense. Which leads to your finding of the sticker that read "The Posse." I guarantee if we go to the lounge and speak to the owner and bartender that was present we can get some info on what type of organization they are. Plus we can see if any cameras outside or inside picked up anything."

Detective Patterson sat down then began writing down the tasks for the day. After he was done he leaned in on his partner.

"Richmond, he's alive," Detective Patterson whispered.

Detective Richmond scrunched her face up at the random act of whispering.

"Huh? What are you talking about? Who's alive?"

"Ssshhh, don't talk so loud right now. Look, the reporters asked about Moretti, and it made me think to tell you he's alive."

"Are you serious? How do you know?"

Detective Patterson glanced across the room to make sure no one was eavesdropping then he went into explanation.

"The night of the funeral I entered my condo and he was sitting on my couch. We had a brief conversation about how it is his destiny to be the top mobster and he even mentioned that our captain is not as clean as we think he is."

Detective Richmond kept a straight face as long as she could. She burst into laughter, causing the other officers to look over into their direction. Detective Patterson didn't find her laughter amusing.

"What's so funny?" he asked with a serious face.

"You're good partner. I mean you almost had me going. Let me ask you this, when did you have this dream?" Detective Richmond asked jokingly.

"I'm not making this up. He even told me he was the middleman that started the whole war between the Jamaicans and the rap crew. Even though I knew it was good confirmation to hear it from him."

Detective Richmond glared at her partner for five seconds, taking everything in before responding.

"So you mean to tell me we went to a funeral and there was nobody in the casket?"

"I mean if you think about it he died in an explosion so there still wouldn't have been a body."

"You're right partner but what does he get out of faking his own death?" Richmond asked inquisitively.

"That's almost a rhetorical question but we are just going to have to sit back and see what's going to happen. I asked myself the same question," Detective Patterson said as he continued.

"Now what I'm really pondering is what type of dirt he has on the Captain."

"No, no, don't go investigating him. We got a fresh case about to start. Don't go ruining it for some other mission."

Detective Patterson chuckled at his partner.

"Look, I need to know and I promise it won't affect the new case."

"Whatever," Detective Richmond said while flagging him at the same time.

Detective Richmond then reached for her plain donut and bit into it. After taking a hefty bite she put it down then stared in her partner's direction while she chewed. Within the brief silence between the two while he was glancing over his notes she could sense that something else was bothering him.

"So did you tell Captain Morello?"

Detective Patterson stopped writing, exhaled, and tossed his pen onto the desk.

"No and I'm still trying to find the right time to."

Right when he was done talking the doors to their department opened and in walked Captain Morello.

"Well now should be a great time," Detective Richmond said with a smirk.

Detective Patterson took a sip of his coffee, rose up, and walked into the direction of his Captain's office. Right before he could make it the desk phone rang, stopping him in his tracks. As Detective Richmond answered he watched her grab a pad, jot down some notes, then hang up, quickly grabbing her jacket and walking in his direction.

"Now's not a good time. We got another body."

Chapter 1

Both Detectives Richmond and Patterson arrived at the scene, which was on Cobbs Creek between Catherine and Christian Streets. When they walked up they watched as the Marine unit and a couple of officers assisted each other with the body of an unidentified female. After acknowledging a couple of officers from their unit they began to ask questions around the scene and they were pointed in the direction of who made the discovery. Standing on the side observing in an all gray Nike jogging suit with his brown bullmastiff on his side, they walked over in his direction to speak to the gentleman.

"Hello sir. I'm Detective Patterson and this is my partner Detective Richmond. Could you please tell us how you made the discovery?"

"Yes, I was on my daily morning jog as you can see that I take my dog with me on. As I approached the area he began to pull me into another direction barking at the same time. He pulled so hard that the chain broke. I ran after him and he led me to the body then I made the phone call."

"Before your jog or during did you witness any cars mysteriously stop in this area?" Detective Richmond asked.

"No, I always jog the same route. And to just let you know I live two blocks away and its traffic nearly 24 hours of the day on this street."

Detective Patterson wrote down in his note pad as the man completed the brief questioning and his partner stepped off to start looking for any other evidence where the body was found.

"Okay thanks sir and thanks for calling," Detective Patterson said as he followed his partner.

While carefully looking over the scene for any clues or lost property that could help them in the case Detective Richmond kneeled down and made a discovery. She picked up the black wallet that had a Chanel symbol on the front of it. She opened it and looked through it, finding a couple of pictures and a State ID hoping that it belonged to the deceased. Detective Patterson came up barehanded from his detection as they both met up to walk over to where the coroner was waiting in the truck.

During the walk over Detective Patterson stopped in his tracks and looked across the street from where they were standing then turned around in the direction of the creek.

"What's up partner? Did we miss anything," Detective Richmond asked as she observed her partner.

"We're going to have to knock on all of those houses to see if they seen any car stop here."

"True, and I say we do that after we come back from the station. Then we could kill two birds with one stone as we make the stop over at the club."

"That's cool with me. Then we could make a stop to get something to eat 'cause a brother is starving," Detective Patterson said while he rubbed his stomach area.

"No problem," Detective Richmond said as they walked over to the coroner.

"Listen, I found a wallet. Fax a copy of this girl's identity once you get prints. I have to make sure it matches what I found inside. Any other discoveries you make a report and notify us," Detective Richmond commanded as her and Patterson walked to his car and drove back to the station.

Detectives Patterson and Richmond walked into the station and headed straight to their desk area, sat down, and began to compare scenarios and notes on what was about to become a second case. To start Detective Patterson pulled out his notepad and Detective Richmond pulled out the wallet she found.

"This wallet has little meaning at the moment until we get the true identity from the coroner's report. But according to the wallet her name is Chanel Cunningham, age 23, and her address is 6624 Lebanon Ave. Now we just sit patiently to see if we have a match."

Detective Patterson nodded in agreement as his partner spoke.

"What else is in the wallet?"

Detective Richmond emptied out the rest of the contents that were inside the wallet.

"Some business cards to a couple of strip clubs. Looks like we can use these for leads. And lastly some pictures of her with two different males."

"So according to these photos and business cards she's a stripper."

"Looks that way partner," Detective Richmond said as she began to pick up the business cards and photos to put back in the wallet.

"Hey, before you put them photos away let me take a look," Detective Patterson said as his perverted tendencies started to arise. "Whoa, not bad at all," he stated, glancing at the photos.

"Oh God please, if you seen one you seen them all," Detective Richmond responded to her partner gawking over the half naked girl in the photos.

Patterson just smiled at his partner's response.

"What a shame. I mean who wouldn't want her to be alive? She's beautiful."

"Obviously somebody didn't want her alive and that's what we need to find out. Now give me back those pictures before you have an accident.

Detective Richmond stopped speaking as Captain Morello stepped out of his office and called out to the both of them to enter immediately.

"Ladies first," Detective Patterson said as he moved to the side to let his partner enter first. Once he entered he already knew to close the door behind him.

They stood side by side waiting to be told they could have a seat once they entered. Captain Morello was staring out of the window with his back facing them. Before he spoke he turned around.

"Good morning Detectives. I won't be long so you two can remain standing," Captain Morello said before turning around then sat down.

Both Patterson and Richmond responded back with Richmond adding a smile to her greeting.

"Now that our morning salutations are out of the way let's get down to business. Two fresh cases on the horizon. Patterson you have the Market Street homicide. Richmond you have the Cobbs Creek case. As always you two can assist each other. I just want these cases closed. Second, IA is going to be conducting interviews the whole week due to the Moretti death. I suggest if it's anything you need to tell them you do so. Now if you have any questions or concerns about what I mentioned please address them now. If not you two are free to go."

Patterson and Richmond turned to look at each other then they responded one by one.

"I have none Captain," Richmond said.

"Same here," Patterson said as they both walked out of his office.

"That was different," Richmond said, as she was the first to sit back down.

Detective Patterson remained standing as he slowly began pacing. He stopped in front of Richmond once he began speaking.

"He's under pressure with the whole Moretti case. See, that's why I want to no more. IA must have already interviewed him and his back is against the wall."

"Don't go jumping to conclusions. Let's stay focused on these cases. As a matter of fact could you busy yourself by getting me some coffee."

Detective Patterson chuckled at his partner treating him like a butler.

"Yes massa I's get you some coffee," Detective Patterson said jokingly.

Detective Patterson returned with two coffees, placing one in front of his partner and keeping one to himself as he sat down.

"Just like you like it; one cream, three sugars."

"I should have said leave it black. It's going to be a long day," Detective Richmond replied before taking a sip.

"So partner, where do we start?" she asked after putting down her coffee.

"I say we swing around the houses and knock on the doors to see if anybody seen anything suspicious. Second on the agenda is to swing past Tony Boy's, get us some breakfast sandwiches, come back to see any evidence came back from the coroner, call them clubs, then last but not least swing past Kif's Lounge."

"Shit, why did I ask? I'm gon' need another cup of coffee."

"I feel you Richmond. It's going to be a long day," Detective Patterson said as they got up to leave and start their investigation.

$$$$

Chase Money woke up breathing like he just finished running a marathon and drenched in his own fluids like he just stepped out of a sauna. He wiped the sweat from his forehead as he gathered his composure sitting on the edge of his king-sized bed. The death of his brother was beginning to haunt him through his dreams. Guilt was running through his bloodstream as he was becoming consumed with getting revenge. The only thing that could settle his bad nerves and thoughts for the moment was some good Kush and a couple shots of Cognac. Since he wasn't an early drinker the Kush was perfect along with popping a Xanax to suppress dealing with his reality sober. Living through a drug haze was how he copped from day to day. Once the high was gone all he could imagine and hear was chaos and a hail of bullets. The rest of the Gwap Gang came to the conclusion that he might need to consider therapy. Jokingly in their smoke sessions they deemed Chase as being classified a Vietnam Vet. Within the joke was some truth. The Gwap Gang went to war and Chance was his war wound but the war had just begun. As he rolled up and took tokes of his high grade marijuana he thought of one person that was going to take long to heal from the ordeal. He just shook his head as he had a random flashback of how his mother was screaming at the sight of both her sons shot and then having to bury one of them. Her words replayed in his head as he exhaled.

"Chase one thing a mom never wants to do is bury one of her own whom she gave birth to."

As he was done with the nostalgia replaying within he decided it would be the perfect time to get dressed and go spend some quality time with his mother. In no time Chase was dressed in a black Polo shirt, black cargos, and a pair of all-black Air Maxes. After getting dressed he grabbed his cell phone and spoke into his phone.

"Call Mom," Chase said, holding his phone two inches away from his mouth. His phone complied and his mother answered on the third ring.

"Hey Chase," his mother answered, sounding groggy as if his call woke her up.

"Did I just wake you up Mom?"

"No. My throat just a little scratchy, that's all. You actually caught me in between starting to cook myself some breakfast."

"Cool, what you cooking? I'm starving," Chase said while he rubbed his stomach.

"I just knew that was coming next. I should've kept my mouth shut. You still ain't find somebody to cook for you in the morning?"

"Nope, not yet mom," Chase said, shaking his head and smiling at the same time.

"Well I guess I can cook for you. I can use the company at the moment anyway."

From the tone of her voice Chase knew that could only mean she had Chance on her mind and was feeling heavy hearted. Chase knew the wounds were still fresh for her too and wanted to put a smile on her face.

"Okay Mom I'm on my way," Chase said as he hung up grabbed his phone charger and keys.

Chase Money pulled up styling on his old block in his black Cadillac STS on cruise control. Some would say when they saw him passing through it was like a presidential motorcade minus the chauffer and entourage. Finally parking he hopped out and was mobbed by a few fans in the hood.

"Yo! Chase what's up? That's ya new ride?" DJ asked while he and his four-man crew came from the Chinese store with bags filled with soda and chips in their hands.

"Yeah young boy, that's my new wheel. You like it?"

"Wow I wanna ride just like this when I grow up."

Chase took a look at all four youths and responded back.

"Listen up y'all. Work hard and you can get whatever you want."

After giving the youngins some brief motivation he pulled out a wad of Benjamin's and spread love around, passing each a yard. His actions sparked a nostalgic moment reminding him how he and his squad were when they were coming up in the hood. All the hustlers used to pass off money to them the same way.

As he was walking towards his mother's house his phone began to ring. As he glanced at his screen he waved his index over the screen then answered.

"Yo Scrilla what's good?

Scrilla on the other end mentioned that he just rode past him and parked up the street on the opposite side by the Chinese store along with Stacks and Paperboi. The only one missing to make the squad complete was Banks.

"Cool, why don't y'all get out and chill with me real quick on my mom porch."

They both hung up as Chase walked upon his mom's porch and waited for the other three quarters of his crew to walk up. One by one they came up on the porch giving Chase handshakes and embraced him slightly as they always greeted each other when in the presence of another.

"You good?" Paperboi asked, as he was the last to come up on the porch.

"Yeah I'm straight, but you know every time I step up here it brings back those memories bro," Chase answered.

Everybody was silent for a brief second, as they all knew losing his brother the way he did was still a hard pill to swallow.

"I know what can snap you out of that," Scrilla said excitingly as he pulled out a vanilla Entourage and a bag of Kush.

"I'm already high bro. Smoked before I left the crib. I'm starving now and y'all niggas ain't helping either

51

with y'all food smelling so good. But that's why I swung past; to eat and chill wit Moms and shit. Where Banks at? Y'all talk to him?"

"Yeah he was hype about something he had to show us for a day now. He said he wanted everybody to be around when he did," Paperboi said, chiming in.

As soon as he was done explaining to Chase, Chase's phone began to ring.

"Speaking of the devil look, this him right here," Chase said as he answered.

"What up bro? Where you at?"

"Riding up Market Street about to get a Tony Boy's sandwich. Where you at?"

"I'm at my mom's crib. It's me and the rest of the squad."

"Cool after I'm done grabbing this breakfast sandwich I'm on my way around there to show y'all this shit."

"Cool well we see you when you get here," Chase said as they both hung up.

"You was right Paperboi. He's hype about something I can hear it all in his voice," Chase said as he rose up and put his cell phone in his pocket.

"Well look, I don't know what y'all bout to get into but I'm about to go in here and get my grub on," Chase said while rubbing his stomach.

Everybody else got up with their food in hand and followed suit except Scrilla. He was the only one hesitant since he was in a rush to smoke the nicely rolled L he was holding.

"You think Moms gon' let me blaze up in the crib?" he asked.

"Now you know Moms ain't going for that shit. Plus you can wait 'til after you eat like the rest of us," Chase said while holding the door open as Scrilla obliged and walked in.

After eating Chase Money and the gang were on the porch smoking and awaiting the arrival of their fellow comrade. Chase Money's phone chimed, notifying him that he received a text message. He checked his message then proceeded to let his homies in on what was up.

"Yo bitches is so funny. Check this out y'all. You remember them bitches we scooped up from the show at the motorcycle club?"

Everybody responded with a hell yeah or a simple yeah as he continued.

"Well the jawn Shannon just hit me up talking about come holla at her. She miss me."

Paperboi being deemed the ladies man out of all of them responded.

"I mean what's wrong with that? That's what they do."

"She's a problem. First time I hit she came at my neck talking 'bout *'Yeah don't think you gon' be getting this pussy all the time, blah blah blah.'* Man when she said that I already knew she was going to be a headache."

"Classic hood shit bro. She just addicted to what the dick did already," Paperboi replied.

Laughter erupted between the crew as they laughed at his response. While enjoying their laughter a man walked up and addressed Chase.

"Yo what's up Mr. Phil? What, you here to see my moms?"

"Yeah what's up youngins?" the 6'2", 200-pound man responded. "I smell that good ol' herb in the air too."

"Herb? Ol' head this that OG Kush," Scrilla said while holding up the L like a trophy.

"Yo chill man. Mr. Phil she in the crib," Chase said as he got up to let him in.

After letting him in the gossiping ensued.

"Yo ya moms dating Mr. Phil dog?" Paperboi asked.

"Yeah man, so what. Moms need to have him around since I moved out and shit. But if it wasn't for him being there moms would probably be in Bellevue somewhere, you dig me?"

"Naw bro, I wasn't coming at you or nothing like that. You know Mr. Phil was in wars and shit. Boy a straight sniper. You know them niggas crazy on the low from all them bodies they be dropping."

Everybody laughed at Paperboi's interpretation of Mr. Phil. Even Chase chuckled but became serious in response back to Paperboi.

"Look as long as he treat my mom right and don't put his hands on her I'm good."

As soon as he was done loud music blared on the block as Banks rolled up playing one their tracks "We Made It," from the EP.

'Bout time this nigga got here," Stacks said as he leaned over and tapped Scrilla for the Kush. "Damn nigga stop being a hoover and pass off."

Banks quickly found a parking space, hopped out, and jogged to the where the rest of the gang was posted up. When he made it to the steps he greeted everybody with a half hug and dap, then he pulled out his phone and pulled up a video on YouTube and handed the phone to Chase. As Chase tapped the play button insults and jabs directed towards them blared through the phone.

"Okay, we gon' start this video right. First off I'm gon' say fuck Gwap Gang. We the real Paperboyz and this is coming from ya boy Pesos. Yeah them niggas got me and my mans in the Chinese store but just to let them know after all that it's on sight when we see them. We gon' take it to them niggas, whether it be on some street shit or this rap shit. Them niggas is straight pussy and we gon' expose them niggas for all y'all Gwap Gang fans. Matter of I'm talking too much. Stop this shit and let's get back to getting money. In the background was his squad with Paperboyz on their shirts and they were holding up pistols and nines. The video didn't even faze Chase Money as he smiled then responded.

"Yo these fake ass niggas out here will do anything for attention. I guess they can't get no attention off their music so they gon' come at us for exposure."

Rants between the squad began as soon as Chase was done speaking.

"Yo I say we go at them niggas and take they heads off verse for verse, 'cause for real ain't nobody fucking with us."

His statement riled everybody else up while Chase remained calm.

"Yeah Banks right. If them niggas want war they can get it just like he said, on sight," Scrilla added with his barbarian like attitude.

"Hold up, hold up. Before anybody else come up with another response let's think before we make this move," Chase said, shutting down the rest of the negativity that was brewing.

"First off, Banks you already know if we go at them that's only making them famous. Second, Scrilla I agree, on sight that's how it's going to go down but we got to remain the unit we always are; five deep and about making money, but ain't nothing wrong with being prepared."

"So what's the move then?" Paperboi asked.

"We remain silent like we didn't even see the video. Silence kills niggas faster than a bullet.

Everybody else stood on the side and nodded in agreement.

"But if they keep coming and our fans take notice then we got to hold down the kingdom we built. But as of right now them niggas is irrelevant.

Everyone agreed by nodding their heads. As Chase was about to receive the Blunt from Banks with his arm extended, two cars pulled up with Caucasian males with black and gray suits. Scrilla and Paperboi, the two who were always strapped for gunplay, gave them no chance of giving them jail time. They ran up the street, leaving Stacks, Chase, and Banks to fend for themselves.

"What's up guys? I'm Agent Daniels. We are here looking for Chase Money and the Gwap Gang."

Chase, Banks, and Stacks looked at each other, waiting for someone to speak up. After the brief seconds of silence and Agent Daniels standing in front of them looking impatient Chase spoke up.

"I'm Chase. How can I help you?

"Well it seems you guys were implicated in a shootout at a popular strip club and we are here to take you in for questioning."

"Well at least can I call my lawyer?" Chase said, pulling out his cell. "Oh yeah and where is this interrogation supposed to take place Officer?"

"We are taking you guys to 6th and Spring Garden, 8th floor."

Chase spoke into his cell after Agent Daniels spoke on the location.

"Scarcetti," Chase said as he waited for his phone to start dialing. The phone rang three times then went straight to voicemail. He then dialed the front desk and a nice pleasant voice answered the phone.

"Hello, this is Cynthia and you've reached the office of the Robert Scarcetti Firm.

"Yo Cynthia this Chase. Is Rob available. I keep calling his phone and he's sending me to his voicemail."

"I'm sorry Chase but he's in a meeting right now. I can take a message for you to leave."

"Good. Tell Robert when he's done meet me down 6th and Spring Garden, 8th floor. I'm being taken in for questioning and I need him to be present."

"Will do Chase. Sixth and Spring Garden, 8th floor," Cynthia said, repeating to make sure she got the right address before they both hung up.

$$$$

"Hello sir, here's your cappuccino," the young brunette waitress by the name of Gia said as she walked up to where Frank was sitting with his eyes glued to the Daily News.

Taking his face away from the paper he replied, "Thanks Gia."

He sipped his cappuccino while watching her swivel her tight ass inside the Levi's she sported. After the brief ass watching he placed his high priced coffee down and began to get back into today's news. His stomach was full after indulging in a breakfast consisting of bacon, eggs, and pancakes, but the main focus of the day was to find ways to solidify himself in the Mobster Hall of Fame. Being connected to the Morettis was where his humble beginnings took place as he was a human sponge soaking everything up he could. Now that he was done shedding the cop life he was all set. He thought about getting his feet wet with petty crimes and hijackings but small time wasn't in his blood. He didn't want to be similar to the old timers. He wanted to jump right in with the sharks. Second on his agenda was to find a crew. He decided to make a posting on Craigslist for cons looking for a job of some sort.

Placing his cell phone down after completing the posting, he got back into browsing the paper. While skimming through he came across an article that raised his eyebrows. It was based on the city contract for laboring municipal vehicles. What else caught his eye was that Moretti was the owner of this contract that was about to expire. City officials already were giving their opinion on how they didn't want a person of his stature with a contract in his hands again. Also some were speculating how he got his signature on there in the first place. The moral of the story was the powers that be were going to make sure this never happened again. An evil grin came over Frank's face as he caught the notion to devise a plan to get his signature on the next contract. He wrote down the contact info for the city official Richard Price who was in charge of contract placements. Next what caught his eye was the long listing of sheriff sales and tax liens. He was always curious about real estate and even thought about taking classes but never took the proper steps to invest the time. He wrote down the contact info for the Sheriff's Office of Gerald Green, which was also located in City Hall. Once writing down that information he noticed that both were in the same location and what better way to kill two birds with one stone? He drank the rest of his cappuccino, got up, left a $50 tip for Gia, and paid his bill.

Once outside he pulled out his pack of Marlboros, tapped the bottom of the pack, and pulled one out, sparking it on the way to his car. His next destination was Boyd's to buy a new suit in preparation for his upcoming business meetings.

Chapter 2

"You know what partner, it kills me when people withhold information that could really help the community in times like this," Detective Richmond said before taking a bite out of her breakfast sandwich. "Oh my God, this sandwich is so good," she said after taking her first bite of her turkey bacon, egg, and cheese on wheat toast.

Detective Patterson chuckled at his partner, knowing she was supposed to be on a diet. He decided to keep that to himself and just reply to her statement.

"I think in this case whoever dropped that body off knew when to do it without anybody being there. Trust and believe if those people would have saw something they would have let us know."

"Yeah so what does that leave us with? A Jane Doe and a wallet we don't even know belongs to her?"

While speaking they didn't notice Captain Morello come striding over.

"Her name is Chanel Cunningham, address 6624 Lebanon Ave. Stripper over at Benji's Playhouse," Captain Morello said, reading off his notepad.

Both Patterson and Richmond had a look of astonishment.

"Her mother was here while you two were gone, she came in and displayed her gratitude. She also wanted to meet the people that were going to be working the case to personally tell them catch the mothafucka' who killed her daughter."

Patterson and Richmond both smiled as Richmond went into her desk pulled out the wallet. She placed the card from Benji's Playhouse and the two pictures Chanel was posing in with two different males.

"I say these are the three leads we go off of at the moment until we find out more info."

"Sounds good. Her mother also left her contact info if you had any additional questions," Morello added.

"Yeah we definitely gon' need to know more on the personal side to solve this case," Richmond said.

After she spoke her and Captain Morello glanced over in Patterson's direction, waiting for him to give his two cents. Richmond couldn't wait any longer and she ended up breaking the ice.

"So I'm curious to what you think partner?"

Patterson looked at the pictures and business card and said the first thing that his brain constructed.

"Follow the ass and cash and we might can solve this case."

Richmond found his statement amusing as Captain Morello just walked back to his office.

"What did I say wrong? You asked and I responded," Patterson said in his own defense.

Shaking her head while still laughing, Richmond responded, "Boy oh boy, you just love to get the Captain riled up. Look, before we go remember we still have to head over Kif's Lounge too, but we can head over to the

Playhouse first so you can get your daily fix of titties and ass," Richmond laughed as she mentioned the latter.

Detective Patterson just shook his head as he rose from his chair.

"Well let's just get this work out of the way and then we can look into you being a comedian later."

Thirty-five minutes later they arrived at Benji's Playhouse.

"It looks closed," Detective Patterson said. He then hopped out his vehicle to confirm.

"Yeah it's closed. I seen the city shutdown papers on the front doors," he said as he arrived back at his car.

"I'm gon' Google to see if there are different locations," he concluded while pulling out his cell phone and going through the prompts. After reading his screen he bookmarked two addresses then proceeded to the first one on 59th and Master.

Arriving about a half hour later the results were the same. The location wasn't open.

"We got one more location Richmond, 54th and Haverford," Patterson said as he headed to that location.

When they arrived at the location it was open. Detectives Patterson and Richmond entered the establishment to find the cleaning crew wiping down the bar and mopping the floor. A husky guard with "security" on his T-shirt came out of the bathroom and greeted both detectives.

"Can I help you?"

Both Patterson and Richmond flashed their badges as Patterson began the conversation with the 300-plus-pound gentleman.

"I'm Detective Patterson and this is my partner. We are here to speak with the owner if he's available."

"Yes he's here. Right this way," the burly man said as they followed him to Benji's office.

The guard knocked and waited for Benji to welcome them in. He knocked once again, and Benji told them to come on in. Being that he was on the phone he quickly dismissed them once he spotted cops entering his office.

"Look I'm going to have to call you back. I got company. Officers, it must be my lucky week. First the Feds now you two. What do I owe your presence too?"

Detective Richmond placed the photos of Chanel on his desk.

"How well do you know Chanel Cunningham?"

"Oh CC, yes she's my number one girl around here. Lines be wrapped around the corner with females and males when they know she's in the building."

"Was," Patterson interjected.

"Wait, wait, what do you mean was bro?" Benji asked as his nostrils began to flare.

"Just like I said, was. She was found dead on Cobbs Creek earlier today."

Benji flopped down in his chair, shocked at the news he just received about his favorite dancer. He took a deep breath then continued.

"So what do you two need to know?"

"Well you can start by telling us who are the men in the photos," Richmond said.

Benji took a glance at the photos then answered.

"Her boyfriend Dawud. If you're wondering if they're two different people looks can be deceiving. He grew a beard."

"Did she mention anything to you about having any beefs of any kind?" Patterson asked.

"Well she did say that he was gung-ho about her quitting the stripper business. That's the only thing I can think of. I run a tight ship so if it was anything else it would've been ran by me."

"Okay so I know this is off subject but I was a fan of your spot on Columbus Blvd. What took place out there for the city to shut you down?" Patterson asked inquisitively.

"I let this rap group shoot a video and do a show there, you know trying to do something different. Somehow there was a shootout in the parking lot, and to make a long story short I'm being sued and the city shut me down until I pay the fines."

"Sorry to hear that," Patterson said like he was concerned about his business. He was only concerned cause he was mad his favorite spot was closed.

"Okay can we get back to why we're here? Sheesh!" Richmond interrupted.

"I have two questions before I'm done. Where were you between the hours of 2 a.m. and 5 a.m.? And did CC work last night? If so what time did she get off and who did she leave with?"

"Not to be smart Detective, but that's more than two questions," Benji said with a grin.

Detective Richmond reached down on her right side and flashed her nine-millimeter and grinned back.

"Whoa. No need to get feisty gorgeous," Benji said.

Patterson laughed at his partner's brashness since he knew she could go from a smile to being a sharp shooter in a matter of seconds. That was one thing he loved about his partner.

"I was here until 3 a.m. and went straight home. But to help you out even more CC wasn't even here. It's Monday; she only works Thursday through Saturday."

"Thanks for your cooperation. Do you have any more questions partner?" Richmond asked as she wrote down some notes on her pad.

"No I think we are done here," Patterson answered as they both stood up.

Both Patterson and Richmond shook Benji's hand and exited the club. As they walked to Patterson's car he still found her actions humorous.

"Were you going to really shoot him for being sarcastic?"

"No I just wanted to let him know I wasn't in a joking mood. But you already know how I play. If the mood strikes I'm not afraid to put a hot one in nobody."

Chapter 3

The next destination for the detectives was Kif's Lounge and they pulled up on Market Street five minutes later, parking in front of the lounge right where they body of Amani was found. After getting out they walked around where his blood stained the concrete hours ago.

"It's a shame how these young guys are losing their lives out here today. Makes you wonder was it that deep to have to take his life," Patterson said while they walked up the ramp to the entrance of the lounge.

"Well partner that's why we're here," Richmond responded as they entered.

The sounds of Bob Marley's "Three Little Birds" could be heard blaring through the clubs speakers, as a man behind the bar sang along with the lyrics swaying in his own world to the Caribbean rhythms.

"Don't worry 'bout a thang 'cause everything little thing is gon' be alright."

"Excuse us!" Patterson interrupted the half grey dreaded man's audition for the next Bob Marley sing-along.

"Sorry brethren, just here cleaning. How can I be of service?" he asked as he grabbed the remote and paused the music.

"Yes I'm Detective Patterson, 18th District. This here is my partner. We are here on behalf of what took place earlier today. Is the owner around?"

"Yes, I'm the owner. The name's Barrington," the six-foot man answered while sticking his right hand out to shake.

He shook the hands of both detectives cordially then walked around the bar as the conversation proceeded.

"So you're here about the murda," he said as his accent took over his words.

"Yes we have a few questions we would like to ask you," Richmond said as she pulled out her pen and pad.

"Let's start with the victim."

"Amani. Good boy. Very tragic what happened to him last night."

"How well did you know the victim?"

"Very well. Him and his crew threw parties here every week. You know the hip-hop/reggae nights."

"Did you know of anybody that would have wanted to kill him?" Patterson followed up from his partner's questions.

"Not really in tune with the business of the underworld. Just stay close to my own officers."

"Okay so let's back it up. Who's his crew?" Richmond asked.

"He's kin to The Kings Men. Very dangerous individuals detectives."

"Yes we already had run ins with The Kings Men," Richmond said while making air quotes.

"So you know that means my name never gets mentioned."

Patterson nodded in agreement.

71

"Me and King we butt heads over the last year or so. For some reason he wants to take over all businesses of the people he helped over here from Kingston. Don't get me wrong I'm thankful for what he did for me and my family, but it was me who started my own business."

"So who attends these events every week?" Richmond asked while jotting down the notes.

"Amani was close to members of The Posse. Both underlings are connected by blood through The Kings Men."

"Now we're getting somewhere. Who's this Posse?"

"They are the offspring of The Kings Men, also from Kingston."

"Is there any bad blood between the two sanctions?"

"Like I said Detective me don't know the underworld business. I just run mines and collect money from them every week."

"Okay surveillance cameras, where are they located?" Patterson chimed in.

"I have three. One in the front, back, and inside the club filming as we speak."

"We would like to view the footage from last night," Richmond asked.

"Right this way," Barrington said as he led them into the back office where the CC TVs were located.

He went into a box labeled archives and pulled out three tapes. The first tape he put in was inside the party. After two minutes of watching Barrington spotted Amani in the crowd by the Jamaican Jacket he wore during the party.

"Here's Amani," he said, pointing at the screen.

He was surrounded by two other males and three women. A man approached him and whispered in his ear, then they laughed and went to the bar ordering drinks and dancing with the females in tow.

"Okay looks like nothing went down inside. Could you fast forward a little?" Patterson asked as Barrington aimed the remote to fast forward the footage.

He began playing it again when The Posse arrived at the event, again pointing out the V.I.P. On tape about half of the party greeted them as they walked through the crowd. Some even passed them beverages as they arrived, showing how much they were respected. About 15 minutes into the tape watching the movements of The Posse, he spotted a male whisper something to another male within the entourage. The male whom received the message walked over to where a female was standing next to where Amani was posted up. He began to pull the female by the wrist and she became agitated. Amani stepped in and by the looks they had a few words and the male walked away. The male walked back over to the dread surrounded by seven other men then whispered something in his ear and that male pulled out his cell phone.

"Okay who's that guy he's whispering to that pulled out his cell phone? 'Cause from what I've seen ever since he walked in the party everybody showed him nothing but respect," Patterson said inquisitively.

"That's Knottie. He runs The Posse."

"Okay he was outside with them same seven men surrounding him when I tried to question them," Richmond said, reminiscing about what happened several hours ago.

"Could you switch to the outside footage?"

"Sure beautiful," Barrington said, causing Richmond to blush.

He popped in the tape and fast forwarded through everybody waiting in line to enter. The Posse entered, then he pressed play when Amani stepped out. His back was against the wall as he was in a blind spot until he stumbled then regaining his balance.

"So from what them three females told me this is when they saw him from across the street in the Chinese store. You can fast forward a little right here," Patterson acknowledged.

"Okay rewind it a little," Patterson said, observing the footage where the perp walked up to Amani.

Barrington rewound then pressed played where the suspect walked up to Amani. Amani passed him the lighter then the assailant pulled out his weapon, let off two shots, and Amani hit the concrete.

"Okay that's all we needed to see. Now if we could match those sequences to the call and him stepping out we

Real

got a suspect on our hands," Patterson said still in observation mode.

Barrington stopped the tape as he watched and listened to Patterson and Richmond talk amongst each other.

"I think you might be right partner. Could you play both again then find out if the times follow the sequence."

Barrington played the tape that was inside the party. When Knottie was on the phone Amani had already stepped out.

"Good observation partner," Richmond said, congratulating her partner.

"What can you tell us about this Knottie character Barrington?"

"Knottie, he's a renegade. Bad news is he will kill for the fun of it."

Richmond put stars by his name, marking the importance of this man.

"Well Barrington thanks for helping us. If we need more we will stop by again," Richmond said warningly.

"Okay detectives, good day," Barrington said after walking them to the entrance for them to exit.

While walking back to the car Richmond's phone chimed as she received a message. She waited until she got in the car and put on her seatbelt to check it. Pressing play on the message Roger and Zapp's "I Wanna Be Your Man" began to play but she quickly paused it to save the embarrassment from her partner.

"Hey why you stop that? That was my jawn right there. I got a lot of pussy from sending jawns that song. Wait, wait, who sent you that?"

"None of your business, that's who," Richmond barked back.

"So you got a stalker on your hands. It's cool. I know I will meet him some day," Patterson said as he pulled out of the parking space.

"You're funny, don't start right now we need to focus on the task at hand," Richmond stated, trying to change the subject.

"Oh okay, well just let my man know that the song sending is played out and he needs to figure a new way in," Patterson said while laughing at his statement.

Detective Richmond just shook her head and laughed at the same time while en route back to the precinct.

$$$$

Topless with black shorts that read "I Love Jamaica" on the rear Simone sat on Knottie's king-sized bed loading up his black Beretta M9, one bullet after the other until the clip was full. After loading up the hollow points she reached for her phone and went into her musical archives, clicked on ganja mix, and pressed play. As the music blared from her Android she began twerking her cheeks to the bass line, catching the eye of Knottie who was counting his earnings for the month. A smile formed on his face as he loved to watch his queen move her ass seductively. He rose up with a stack of Benjamins clutched in his right hand walked over and smacked her left cheek then placed the greenbacks in his pocket.

"Spark up," he demanded, plopping on his back.

Simone grabbed the green ashtray with a perfectly rolled Backwood full of the finest ganja. King put him in charge of growing his new product that he was sending by the seed. A couple of puffs of this plant for the average smoker left them with a serious cough, blood shot eyes, and a high for at least four hours. It was the best quality money could buy and Knottie had an unlimited supply on a daily basis.

Simone sat on top of his pelvis area with a lighter and the Backwood in her possession. She flicked the lighter and brought it to the tip and took two huge puffs. Tossing the lighter to her left side she tilted her head slightly to the right and exhaled, causing a cloud to form. Smiling at Knottie who had both of his arms extended caressing her firm breasts, she began to wind to the tunes once again, after taking another puff and exhaling she turned the Blunt around in her mouth. With her index she signaled Knottie to rise, and as they met face-to-face she began to blow and he sucked like a hoover. He exhaled then laid back on his spine, admiring Simone as she swiveled her hips to the music. Their smoke session came to a halt once Knottie's phone began to ring. He glanced at his iPhone screen then started snapping his finger and pointing towards Simone's phone for her to cut off the music. She quickly grabbed her phone, hitting the pause button then he answered.

"Blessings King."

"No Blessings. I have no peace right now. My mind is at war," King said on the other end.

Knowing he was angry and probably received the news of Amani losing his life Knottie brought on some assurance.

"He who killed Amani is going to die a thousand deaths."

"Knottie. Along with the ganja business I gave you one simple task and that was to watch after my negotiator until I got back. Now he's dead."

"Apologies King. Accept my apologies."

"Don't apologize no more. Next time I give you a task like that you don't fuck it up. Now I need you to take care of the deeds. All I need is two more; The Happy Inn and Kif's. The rest will fall in place once I get back."

"When do you want me to go meet with the owners?"

"ASAP. They probably will be expecting Amani, but I will call them back and let them know there will be a new enforcer coming."

"Okay King, I will not let you down again. You have my word brethren."

"Your life depends on that word Knottie. And that's not a threat, that's a promise so don't fuck up."

King left him with those last words of sincerity then hung up.

"What did he say?" Simone asked while trying to read Knottie's facial expression at the same time. Knottie sparked the Backwood that went out during the conversation, took a long pull, then exhaled.

"He gave me the green light. The Posse has the power now."

$$\$\$\$\$$

Both Detectives Patterson and Richmond entered the front entrance of the District to address the dispatcher Debbie Owens. Officer Debbie was a light-skinned, thick, wide-hipped officer who loved her donuts and coffee but never let her frequent snack breaks get in the way of her diligence. As they approached the window she was reading the latest Ebony magazine.

"Hey Officer Owens, could you do us a favor? We need a printout of a perp by the name of Knottie," Detective Patterson said as he passed her a piece of paper with his name on it.

"Hey! Whatever for my favorite detectives. I can have this in no time. Have a seat and I will be right back."

Patterson and Richmond sat on the lobby bench along with the raw stench of five-day-old piss from the homeless people that frequented the lobby of the precinct after hours.

"Ugh! Do we have to sit here? It smells like we sitting in a sewer."

Detective Patterson chuckled at his partner's humor.

"It won't be long. All she has to do is pull up his name in the system and print it out."

Detective Richmond ignored her partner and pulled out her Chanel No. 5 and sprayed it in the air.

"There, that should help for the moment," she said after putting her perfume back in her bag.

Detective Patterson shook his head as Officer Owens came back to the window and slid him the printout of Knottie's history.

"Thanks babe," Detective Patterson said as he received the paperwork.

"Always a pleasure," Officer Owens spewed back with a wink.

"Well, well, looks like we're on to something. Ya boy Knottie hasn't been the utmost citizen in West Philadelphia. He doesn't have a long rap sheet but it's viable enough to go after him. Two misdemeanor charges of marijuana possession and one felony charge of an illegal firearm with the intent to sell for which he received probation. He's still on probation according to that charge, and I guarantee being connected to King his probation officer has been paid off to leave him alone."

"Of course. You know some people get the cash payoff to turn the other cheek," Detective Richmond added.

As soon as she was done speaking a tall dark-skinned woman walked inside the lobby, eyes bloodshot from crying and looking like she just stepped out of bed with her pajamas on. When she spotted both detectives staring she walked over and began to plead her presence.

"Officers I have a problem on my hands and I need your assistance."

"Speak your peace ma'am," Richmond said.

"Yes my name is Darnice and I would like to file a missing person's report. I also have pictures of my daughter."

After speaking she passed the two photos to Detective Richmond before she sat down on the bench and began sobbing, wiping her tears away with an already overused tissue. Detective Patterson walked over and began to console her and discuss the issue.

"Everything is going to be okay. We are here to help, and I'm sure we are going to find her. May I ask how old is she?"

"She's 23."

After answering she began to rant and stomp her right foot.

"I told her, I told her to stop. Please Lord! Please Lord tell me my child is okay. Please Lord!

"Ma'am try to calm down. What is her name and what did she do?"

Darnice raised her head up wiped away the excess tears then began to answer Detective Patterson.

"Well sir Deseree is going to CCP to become a nurse. Once enrolled she began to hang around this girl named Mocha. I mean I can spot a whore when I see one. You know the long weave and the pants that show off your ass crack along with the lower back tattoo. My daughter was raised to be a standup Christian. I guess the allure of fast money got a hold of her soul along with the serpent tongue of Mocha."

While she was deep into explanation Richmond tapped Patterson, showing him a picture with the same guy that was in the photo with Chanel a.k.a. CC.

"Darnice could you please tell me the name of this male in the picture with your daughter?"

Darnice snatched the picture glanced at it then passed it back to Patterson.

"That loser's name is Dawud. She's always coming to me crying about them arguing about their relationship, mentioning the fact that he always wanted her to quit dancing and he would take care of her. I keep telling her he only wants her for sex. My baby is book smart but sometimes she can be very naïve."

"Well do you suspect he has something to do with her being missing?" Patterson asked.

"Who knows? I'm not going to jump to conclusions but I wouldn't put it past that scumbag."

"Do you have a last name for the scum, I mean Dawud?"

"Yes. Dawud King."

"Okay thanks," Patterson said as he walked over to Officer Owens.

"Owens I'm going to need another print up. The name is Dawud King."

Officer Owens stopped reading her magazine and hopped up to get his paperwork.

While Patterson waited at the window Richmond attended to the grieving mother.

"Did you stop past her house to see if she was there?" Richmond asked.

Darnice raised her head to address Detective Richmond.

"What's your name officer?"

"Detective Richmond. You can call me Natasha too."

"I will call you Detective. Now that we got that out of the way Detective what's your faith?"

"I was raised Christian but since becoming engulfed in work I haven't been practicing my faith as I should."

"Well what you seek you shall find. I don't fear nothing but the Lord, but right now I feel like if I go seeking for my daughter she will be dead. I've been sitting in the house for the last three days waiting for her to call me only to just to receive calls from my mother."

Well Darnice I agree with you, but how are you going to have any type of peace if you don't find out where she is?"

Darnice took a deep breath then answered Richmond.

"You know what Detective, you're right. Let's go. I'm sure she's okay. She probably got caught up with that dirty nigga."

Darnice and Detective Richmond rose up from the bench and walked over to the window where Patterson received the paperwork on Dawud.

"Look partner, I'm going to run over to Deseree's house with her Mother. I guess from the info you received you can find out where we can find this Dawud character."

"Okay well I will be here until you two come back," Patterson said as his partner and Darnice walked out of the precinct.

Chapter 4

Detective Richmond and Darnice parked in front of Deseree's house on Locust between 54th and 55th Streets.

"That's her house right there," Darnice mentioned, pointing to the house with 5450 on the front.

It was adjacent from the low-income apartments that stretched from 55th to 54th. Residents sat on the front steps with their children running rampant up and down the block while they indulged in the vices of Newports, marijuana, and alcohol.

Both Richmond and Darnice got out of the car and proceeded to go inside. Once they reached the entrance Detective Richmond checked to see if there was any forced entry.

"I have a key detective," Darnice mentioned while reaching into her purse.

"You don't need it," Richmond said as she turned the knob with her suit jacket sleeve.

"That's not like her to leave her front door unlocked. She never trusted these hooligans running around on this block," Darnice said as she watched Richmond walk in and pull out her nine from her waist.

"You might wanna wait out here until I let you know the coast is clear."

Darnice ignored her orders and walked inside behind Richmond.

"Detective Richmond I fear nothing but the Lord. I'm coming in with you."

Detective Richmond didn't want to argue with her so she let her come along. The first room they entered was the living room. A black leather sectional graced the wall, along with a glass table full of the latest hip-hop magazines. On the wall in front of the sofa was a 50-inch flat screen, which was still on. The menu prompts for Jason's Lyric were on the screen. Strong marijuana fumes filled the living room as Richmond followed the scent into the kitchen where she found an ashtray with a half smoked Entourage along with a perfectly rolled Entourage, a dime bag, and two more cigars in the package. Richmond made a mental note of the smoke session and the empty bottle of pink Moscato. A thump startled her as she pointed her gun then called out to Darnice.

"Darnice!

Darnice didn't respond to Richmond's call so she crept up the stairs, gun pointed just in case there were some unexpected guests still on the premises. When she made it to the top of the steps she made a right into the master bedroom to find Darnice on her knees praying, sounding like she was speaking gibberish. Richmond heard this before as she remembered that's how some people sounded when in prayer. On the bed is where Deseree laid on her stomach, eyes still open as sheets covered the bottom half of her body.

Richmond pulled out her cell phone to contact the district.

"Yes this is Detective Richmond. I'm at 5450 Locust Street and I'm in need of a coroner, C.S.I, and call my partner Detective Patterson. Tell all of them to meet me here as soon as possible."

$$$$

Detective Patterson and the coroner arrived at the same time. As he pulled up behind them on the corner of 55th and Locust he slid his cell out of his waistband and called Richmond to let her know they were on the premises. Detective Richmond met up with them at the front entrance and directed the coroner to make their way upstairs to where Deseree's body lay lifeless.

"Listen, before you go her mom is still in there praying so just be mindful of her presence."

Once they made their way upstairs Detective Richmond guided her partner into the kitchen to discuss evidence.

"So when CSI gets here I got to inform them there was more than one person inside this house. You got the Moscato bottle, two glasses, and I guarantee fingerprints and DNA are all over them. Also saliva on the half smoked Blunt over here."

"Hell yeah partner. Now the question is whose DNA?"

"Good question Patterson. I'm leaning more towards the so-called boyfriend."

Patterson stood in silence for a few seconds then answered.

"Who Dawud? The man she mentioned at the precinct?"

"Yes he should be the number one suspect. He's already been implicated in both murders. I say that's one too many."

"You got a point partner. But I wouldn't rule out Mr. Benji either. Two strippers earning a lot of money for him. Maybe they wanted to really leave cause of "their boyfriend." You know how the game goes. People become obsessed and that's when murder comes into play."

Richmond pondered on her partner's words as they walked out of the kitchen back into the living room.

"Hmmm. Valid point, so we have our top suspects. All we need is that physical evidence, then I'm sure we will find our murderer."

Once Richmond stopped talking the sounds of Darnice coming downstairs caught their attention as both detectives turned around. She walked upon them and spoke.

"Detectives all I want is justice. Find my daughter's murderer so I can be at peace."

Detective Richmond reached out and placed her right hand on top of Darnice's shoulder.

"We are going to need your help but we promise we will find who did this to your daughter."

Chapter 5

Chase Money exited the doors to the building with full force. He was pissed off due to being stuck in interrogation for hours without eating and the urge of getting high was at an all time high.

"Chase, Chase," Scarcetti yelled out before Chase, Banks, and Stacks walked away.

His hair slicked back and his Tom Ford suit tailored to perfection, Scarcetti walked in Chase's direction once he saw that Chase wasn't turning back. Once he caught up to them he began to talk.

"Look Chase, I know they had you in there for a long duration but listen, there's holes in this case that I can plug up. All charges will be dropped. I promise."

"Don't promise us anything. We are not keen on promises. Just make it happen," Chase said as he looked directly into his lawyer's eyes.

Chase, Stacks, and Banks stood in silence staring at Scarcetti after Chase spoke, waiting for his response. After the brief stare down Scarcetti bought on some closure.

"Give me a few days and we will be popping the finest champagne celebrating victory."

Chase nodded then spoke.

"I can dig that. Just make it happen Scarcetti. That's what we pay you for."

The conversation ended then they parted ways with Scarcetti walking to his black Bentley Azure and Chase and the rest of the squad walking towards the El.

"What's the move now bro?"

Chase Money looked over at Banks while en route to the Spring Garden stop.

"Get with Scrilla and Paperboi to discuss this issue and get something to eat 'cause a nigga is starving."

"You got a spot in mind?" Banks asked.

"Yo we should go to the Happy Inn. The food and drinks are good and we need something like that in our lives after being up in that building all day," Stacks interjected.

"Cool, sounds like a plan. First we got to hit up Scrilla and Paperboi and tell them to meet us on the block."

After making it to Front and Spring Garden they heard the train arriving so they sprinted up the steps and Chase dropped a ten dollar bill. They barely made it as a passenger held the door for them. The train pulled from the stop as they took their seats and Chase reached into his pocket, withdrawing his cell phone and quickly calling Scrilla before the El made it underground.

"Yo Chase what's up? Me and Paperboi was waiting for y'all call. What happened? Scrilla said as he answered.

"We on our way back around the way. We will tell you all about it when we get there. We on the El and about to go underground. Once we hit 46th Street I will hit you back."

Chase hung up right before the El could reach underground and rested his head on the window to quietly enjoy the brief ride as thoughts swirled around his head about the direction his squad was going in.

The El train came to a complete stop on 56th and Market as the doors opened and passengers exited. Being that it was crowded Chase Money, Banks, and Stacks didn't want to risk being spotted so they decided to fall back before the doors closed to be the last passengers to walk off. Plans of trying to be incognito failed when a fan spotted them.

"Oh my God! Chase Money, come here. What you doing on the El? Please we have to take a picture so I can post it on my Instagram."

Luckily the other pedestrians were ignoring the excitement the 22-year-old female was giving off. She sported a tight all-black one-piece, red lipstick, red and black #5 releases from Jordan, and gold bamboo earrings. Her hair was bobbed to perfection. She pulled Chase over to the nearest empty space held out her phone in the air and posed while Chase held up a peace sign then she snapped the picture. After taking the picture Chase admired the young girl's attributes, which were nice and tight as her vagina print stuck out like a camel toe.

"Look shorty, I got business to attend to. Now if I didn't then you would be rolling wit me tonight. But before I roll let me get ya number so we can go out sometime."

A huge grin formed on the young girl's face while she stared up at Chase.

"Okay and my name is not shorty, it's Aquilla."

Chase chuckled at the fact he was being put in his place.

"Damn youngin' it ain't even that serious."

"I was just letting you know plus you asked for my number before asking my name."

Chase nodded in agreement. Aquilla then gave him her number and Chase stored it in his phone.

"Okay cool, now that I got your name and number I will holla at you later."

As Chase and the rest of the crew started to walk towards Chestnut, Chase's phone began to ring.

"Yo Scrilla," Chase said answering.

"Where y'all at? Niggas over here getting restless," Scrilla said on the other end.

"Chill, we just hopped off the El and I ran into a fan. We walking down 56th. We just crossed Chestnut."

"Cool, hurry up cause I just got finished rolling up."

Chase, Banks, and Stacks walked up on Scrilla and Paperboi who were posted up on Scrilla's all-black Dodge Magnum. Scrilla and Chase embraced then Scrilla passed him the Kush he lit up before they walked up. Chase took a long pull then exhaled as Scrilla sparked conversation.

"So what them boys want?"

After taking another long pull Chase exhaled then answered.

"First off you two niggas is lucky y'all jetted up the block when they pulled up. They had us in separate rooms cooped up trying to sweat us out talking about an investigation. Come to find out that nigga Benji caught the feet under his chin syndrome."

Everybody was puzzled but laughed at the same time.

"What the fuck is feet under the chin syndrome'? Paperboi asked.

"It means that nigga is running his mouth," Chase explained.

"Well what you expect? He ain't bout that life," Banks added.

"Well it don't matter 'cause we got to go holla at him to see what this whole case is about. Plus we got to go hard and get our money up even more so we can pay Scarcetti."

"Man this shit crazy. We get shot at and now we fighting for our freedom," Scrilla said.

"Yeah seems that way bro," Banks answered while receiving the Kush from Chase.

"Now as far as money Chase you know we been sitting on the pounds of Kush that dirty cop gave us to move," Banks interjected.

Hope formed in Chase's demeanor in a form of a smile.

"Oh shit Banks, I'm glad you reminded me about them. Now where were they stashed at?"

"I kept them at my crib. I ain't gon' lie though I was tempted to pinch some and smoke but I didn't.

"I'm glad you didn't," Chase said with sincerity.

"Thing is we have been disconnected from the streets since going hard with the music and shows so who we gon' sell them to?" Stacks asked.

"Stacks for hustlers like us it's in our veins. There is no such thing is being disconnected. We are always connected," said Chase.

After speaking to Stacks Chase's phone chimed as he received a text. While checking the text and texting back, Banks and Scrilla began discussing a plan they always wanted to be in motion but never had the opportunity until now.

"What's up with getting our hands on some white girl?" Scrilla asked.

"Man 54th is opened up. I say it would be the perfect time to move in on that," Banks answered.

"Cool, I like the sound of that. All we need is a connect," Scrilla added.

Chase was on the sideline acting as if he was texting and not ear hustling but he heard every word.

"Why would y'all want to put the whole squad in jeopardy? We not drug dealers. I mean I know we move Kush here and there but that's just to ball out on. But now y'all over here talking 'bout coke."

"Listen, we talking 'bout coming up, that's all. Ain't nothing wrong with coming up," Paperboi said.

"Right now we hot. Feds on us for that shootout and I'm not trying to invest in nothing like that so they can add drug charges to that."

Everybody was silent once Chase brought up the Feds again.

"Look, let's just roll out. We can talk about this shit later," Chase added.

Everybody agreed as the Kush was tossed and everybody was on the verge of catching the munchies.

"Where y'all trying to go tonight?" Scrilla asked.

"Let's go to the Happy Inn. The hos is always in there," Paperboi acknowledged.

"Cool let's mob out now 'cause I got some pussy lined up for later," Chase said.

"Uh-huh, that's why you was texting all crazy, Banks said.

"You already know," Chase said as they slapped their hands twice while walking to his Caddy.

Chapter 6

Cruising through the city blocks the Gwap Gang reached their destination in 15 minutes taking the scenic route of Cobbs Creek. Two cars deep they hopped out in unison and proceeded to the entrance of The Happy Inn. While entering Chase Money's phone chimed for the 15th time.

"Yo this bitch been blowing my phone up ever since we was on our way here."

"She a stalker bro," Scrilla answered

"Man tell her to fall back. You chillin' wit the squad," Banks also replied.

Chase Money ignored their comments and stepped to the side while the rest of the gang walked through the metal detector and greeted their favorite security guard. After Chase was done texting he walked through the metal detector and greeted him as well.

"What's up D?" Chase said while shaking the hand of the burly brown-skinned man with a Sunni beard.

After the brief embrace D replied back, "Nothing much man. What y'all doing here tonight? Y'all usually come on Friday or Saturday."

"We just wanted to step out for a minute and grab something to eat and drink. Plus my man's said it be jumping on a Monday."

A smile formed on D's face as he responded, "Oh okay, ain't nothing wrong with that. It do be jumping on Mondays but that's later on around like 11 or 12 a.m."

Chase Money glanced at his pricey timepiece before responding.

"That's like two hours from now so I don't even know if I'm gon' witness that. We'll see D."

Chase walked away from D to catch up to the rest of the gang who were posted up in the rear ordering food. After ordering their four chicken wing and fried rice platters they stepped to the bar to start the beginning of their alcohol consumption.

"Shots of Patron Lime sound good right now," Banks blurted out as they stood around trying to figure out to what to drink.

As they pondered Jasmine the bartender stood in front tapping her fingernails on the bar awaiting their decision.

"Patron sounds good," everyone agreed.

"It took y'all long enough," Jasmine said.

"Man don't worry 'bout all that. Just make it five doubles," Banks said, pulling out a knot of 100s and 20s.

"Fifty dollars" Jasmine said while holding her hand out.

Banks handed over $60 and told her to keep the change. After receiving the money and thanking him for the tip Jasmine pulled out five shot glasses, placed them on top of the bar, and began pouring until five shots were completed.

"Okay y'all grab ya shots. This is for that bullshit case the Feds think they got and to all out haters coming for our crown," Banks said while raising his shot.

Everyone else followed suit and raised their shot then swallowed. After taking the shots Chase's phone chimed again. He grew annoyed even before checking it since he thought it was the culprit that has been blowing up his line for the last half hour. Once he checked it he was shocked to see it was Streets telling him to call him ASAP.

"Ayo! That wasn't the jawn. It's Streets."

"Man what the fuck that nigga want after filming them other niggas coming at us. He should go on the shit list along with Benji," Banks blurted out.

"He probably trying to plead his case. I'm gon' step in the bathroom and call this nigga."

Chase stepped away from the bar and proceeded to the bathroom. After making his way past a couple of patrons playing pool he made his way to the bathroom. Once inside he pulled out his cell, went into his call list and found Streets, and pressed his screen to call him.

"What's good Chase?" Streets answered on the other end.

"You tell me Streets," Chase said as he began to pace back and forth.

"I know y'all probably saw the video but just let me start by saying that was for ratings bro. You know how niggas love controversy."

"Look Streets, right now I ain't trying to hear that. You got the squad ready to come take ya head off."

"Come on Chase, no need for all that. Look, y'all wear the crown right now and it was only a matter of time before niggas was gon' come and snatch it. Plus it's only business. The streets is waiting for y'all to reply."

Chase stopped pacing then responded.

"Naw no reply. We gon' kill them niggas with silence. It ain't like they on our level with the music anyway. Them niggas just mad about what happened in Danny Wok."

"Well look I don't know about all that beef shit. I just know ya fans is waiting just like I am. Maybe y'all can do something like a brief response or something," Streets said, trying to be persuasive."

Chase stood still and pondered for a brief second then answered.

"Let me get back to you on that Streets 'cause we got bigger fish to fry right now them niggas is guppies to us."

"Okay cool Chase, not trying to pressure you into doing something you don't want to do but just get back to me when y'all ready to make some more moves."

"Cool Streets, I got you," Chase said as they both hung up.

As soon as Chase hung up and exited Beenie Man's "Rum and Red Bull" began to blast through the bar speakers. Observing that the crowd grew in size, the dance floor filled up with females winding and chanting to the lyrics. Chase made his way back to the bar. Banks and Stacks stood by the bar awaiting his arrival. As he approached him Banks spoke after taking a sip from the Yuengling in his possession.

"So what that nigga was talking about?"

"Man the usual business but he said he didn't do it to go against us. He did it to spark a little controversy to bring in more money."

"Man I ain't tryin' to hear that business shit. I'm ready to ride on them niggas, point blank."

"I feel you Banks, but let's think before we move. That's all I'm saying. You never know a niggas motive behind the moves they make. We got to stand back and let niggas reveal their true selves. In a minute we gon' see how much loyalty Streets has to our movement."

Chase paused for a second then continued to speak.

"He did make a point though Banks. He mentioned we on top and they trying to knock our crown off."

"And that's why I say we crush them niggas just in case they catch us slipping."

Chase stood in silence taking in the atmosphere. Scanning the room from his left and right peripheral's for the rest of his entourage.

"Where's Paperboi and Scrilla?"

"Once Paperboi and Scrilla peeped the jawns going to the dance floor, well you know the rest," Stacks said as he made his way to the pool table area.

After they spoke on the whereabouts of everybody in the lounge Chase tapped Banks for them to make their way to the dance floor area to peep the scenery. The DJ was already on his second song of the night as RDX's "Bend Ova" echoed throughout the lounge. Making their way through the slightly crowded area they spotted Paperboi and Scrilla grinding on two females. The two females had their hands planted on the floor along with their asses in the air with black tops with sweatpants to match that had the Jamaican flag on them. As they swiveled their butt cheeks to the beat Scrilla and Paperboi were enticed to grind on them harder.

"So this is how it is on a Monday," Chase blurted out to Banks who along with everybody else was on the side spectating.

"This jawn is jumping," Banks retorted as he turned to his right in the direction of the pool tables.

"Look at Stacks. He probably over taking niggas money. Let's go over and see what he up to," Banks said to where Stacks was in position to shoot the eight ball. He struck the cue ball and made it curve in the middle of the table as it struck the eight ball and the eight ball went into the side pocket. After making the shot he walked over to where a dark-skinned male in all black sipping on a Guinness stood with aggression building on his face. His face grew tighter as he went into his pocket and pulled out a fifty-dollar bill and passed it to Stacks. Stacks snatched the fifty and left the man with some words of wisdom about betting.

"Look, I told you should've never bet me. I'm nice with the stick homie. Now you over there with the tight face."

Banks and Chase Money just stood on the side laughing at how the man's face scrunched up from losing his money.

"Bet it back and double it," the man responded aggressively.

Stacks shrugged then counteracted.

"Cool wit me. Y'all niggas gon' watch me take this nigga bread?"

Banks and Chase looked at each other then Chase replied.

"Naw man, we going back to the bar and then we on the dance floor 'cause that's where all the hos is at."

They turned around and made their way back to the bar where Chase ordered a coconut Ciroc and pineapple mix while Banks grabbed another Yuengling and a shot of Patron Lime. After Banks took back his shot they walked over to D as he stood by the metal detector awaiting the arrival of more patrons. As they loomed Banks was the first to speak.

"Yo D, what's up with all the Jamaican music?"

"Oh y'all must don't know Mondays is reggae nights."

Banks and Chase both looked at each other as Chase countered D's response.

"Yo tell me you're joking."

D grinned then responded.

"No, listen to the music. They might toss in a little hip-hop but 95% of the music is gon' be reggae."

At the sight of Chase's and Banks' expressions D became curious.

"What's up, why y'all tripping? It's a lot of females in here and you know how them Jamaican jawns move they asses."

Banks laughed at D's description while Chase kept his composure and explained the situation.

"Look D, I don't know if you heard but we went at it with a couple of Jamaicans not too long ago, that's all."

D's whole demeanor changed when he realized the sincerity in Chase's voice.

"Oh okay, understood. Well y'all surely don't want to be up in here then. You might come across them niggas you went head up with. Our spot brings people from the whole tri-state."

Right after D spoke Chase's phone began ringing. He pulled it out and just glared at it without answering and shook his head. Banks laughed then spoke.

"Man I know who that is. You might as well answer."

Chase let out a fake laugh then spoke.

"Fuck you nigga. But you right, this bitch has been blowing my phone up from the time we were on our way here from the time we got here and now look. She is relentless."

"Yo what's up?" Chase answered in an aggressive tone.

"Nigga what's taking you so long and where are you at wit all that music in the background?"

Chase removed the phone away from his face and addressed D and Banks who were already spectating.

"This bitch act we married or something."

Banks and D laughed at Chase's remark.

"Listen me and my niggas stopped to get a drink and some food at the Happy Inn. I was gon' hit you up after we was done."

"Oh okay Chase, well do that, and could you get me something to eat and two vanilla wraps?"

"Okay cool," Chase said as he hung up.

"I can't stand impatient bitches bro. All they want is your time and don't know what to do with it when they get it."

Banks and D laughed at Chase once again as two other security guards Reg and Tyson sprinted over to D.

"Yo D we got two situations," Reg said almost out of breath.

Chase Money and Banks shadowed Reg, Tyson, and D to the dance floor. Once D and Reg cleared everyone out the music cut off and lights came on. Paperboi and Scrilla walked over to Chase and Banks with their faces balled up yelling obscenities.

"What's going on?" Chase inquired.

Scrilla spoke on the situation.

"While we were dancing with the freaky Jamaican jawns these two little niggas came out of nowhere drawling talking 'bout this is the boss man lady. You know me, I wasn't trying to hear that so I mugged the shit out that nigga and we started to scuffle a little."

Banks instantly burst into laughter at Scrilla. D walked up on all four of them while they stood deliberating their next move.

"Listen, I think it would be wise if y'all just left so nothing else goes down," D said sincerely.

"That's cool D. We missing one more out of the squad. Where's Stacks?" Chase asked before they began walking to the exit.

As Chase spoke on is whereabouts he appeared strolling from the direction of the pool tables. His face was balled up from hostility.

"What's good bro?" Banks asked.

"That Wesley Snipes looking ass nigga was about to have me smack the shit out of him with a pool stick. He wasn't trying to give me my bread. Ol' nut ass niggas, I swear."

Chase and the rest of the squad laughed at Stacks while exiting, only to remain out front. Once outside Chase automatically remembered he didn't get his food he ordered. He banged on the exit door and luckily D was right beside it as he stepped out.

"What's up Chase? You know I can't let you back inside."

"Look D, I forgot to get my food. Here's my ticket."

As Chase began to pass him his ticket everybody else's brain caught up and remembered they didn't have any food either. Before D could go back in he received four more tickets.

Awaiting the arrival of their food Paperboi broke the silence with his belligerence.

"Yo I'm ready to go back in there and smash all them niggas," he spoke, raising his neck in the air.

Chase shook his head at how he was still oblivious to what really happened.

"Who the fuck were they?" he asked while everybody stood around.

"I don't know. All I know is like I told you one of them dreads walked up and said this boss man lady. You know I wasn't trying to hear that shit. All I know is shawty had a fat ass and I was on it."

Everybody cackled at Paperboi because they knew he was being sincere. He was the type to be so impulsive even if a girl said she had a boyfriend he would still chase they pussy.

Chase began to drift off deep in thought. Banks caught the same energy then spoke.

"You thinking what I'm thinking Chase?"

Chase glanced at his right hand then responded.

"It all depends on what you thinking."

"It's just funny those niggas could be the same niggas that had something to do with Chance's murder."

Chase quavered his head at the scenario Banks uttered unto him.

"You might be right but I don't even want to think on that level right now 'cause I would burn down this whole lounge if I thought an ounce of that true. All I can think about right now is eating and getting some pussy. As matter of fact what's taking D so long getting our food?"

Scrilla smacked his teeth at Chase mentioning of pussy.

"Damn nigga do you got to rub it in like that?"

Laughter erupted between the camp as Chase spoke in between.

"Yo this nigga act like he don't get the most pussy out of all of us."

"You right Chase. Thanks for reminding me. Let me scroll through my phone right now."

After Scrilla spoke and pulled out his cell D came out and distributed the food.

"Good looking out D. Hopefully the next time we come through it be more peaceful on our behalf. You know what I'm sayin'?"

D nodded to Chase then responded back.

"Yeah I hear you Chase. You know how it is in this city. You gotta be prepared for any and everything."

D went back inside and left the Gwap Gang, who already determined their next location would be 56th and Walnut.

Chapter 7

Parking in front of the Chinese store, Chase hopped out and went inside and purchased two vanilla Entourages and two lemonade iced teas. Exiting the store with his items for his nightcap with Shannon he walked up on his family to say his goodbyes as everyone was posted up along their cars consuming their food. With a mouth full of fried rice and chicken wings Banks spat a few words to his partner in crime.

"Yo you might as well chill with us. Fuck that bitch for tonight. You know we got to discuss how we gon' get this bread for Scarcetti."

Chase disregarded Banks' request to shutdown his thirst for intercourse.

"Yo this bitch been hitting me for the longest and I want some pussy bro. You know I'm not the one to chase it so when it presents itself like this I take it."

Everybody else laughed on the sideline because they knew Chase Money wasn't lying. His name fit him to a T. All he desired to do was Chase Money. Females took a back seat to that.

"You not listening to me Chase. Stop thinking with your third leg. I'm serious."

A huge grin formed on Chase's face before responding.

"I'm serious too and right now I can't hear you for the simple fact my balls are filled up and I got to shoot that load off."

The rest of the gang burst into laughter. Scrilla fell on the hood of Banks' all-black Dodge Charger and Paperboi almost dropped his platter. Stacks still laughing with a Joker type grin on his face, walked over to mediate.

"Yo let the little nigga breathe homie," Stacks said while leaning on Banks' shoulder.

Banks nudged him off his right shoulder then went into a rant.

"If this nigga was good right now he would be trying to get rid of that work we got left over and focus on tying up these loose ends."

Banks wiped the smirk off Chase's face as Stacks was about to approach Banks for smacking his arm of his shoulder. Chase raised his arm between them.

"I got this Stacks. So what you saying I ain't focused. C'mon man, don't ever try and play me like that. I'm always focused. Let me breathe for a minute. We gon' have time to handle everything."

Banks who almost reached his boiling point was still mad but he fell back.

"Cool Chase, my bad bro. I'm just a little frustrated from earlier my nigga."

"Naw it's cool you don't even have to apologize. I appreciate you bringing up that work. We can find somebody to buy it all, plus like you said figure out how to tie up them loose ends."

Banks and Chase embraced after their minuscule confrontation.

"Enjoy that pussy bro. I guess me and the rest of the squad gon' fall—"

Scrilla interrupted Banks in mid sentence.

"Shit I'm on the same page as Chase. I ain't gon' miss the opportunity to be laid up."

Everybody chuckled at Scrilla as Chase pulled out his phone to call Shannon.

After three rings she answered.

"About time nigga. What you on your way?"

Chase shook his head at the sound of her being impatient.

"Yeah man, I'm on my way."

"Don't sound like that boo. Did you buy what I asked for?"

"Yeah, damn. Look, I'm hanging up."

Chase hit the red button and just shook his head, one of his favorite motions after being aggravated.

"Impatient, ungrateful ass bitches. I don't even know why I'm being bothered now."

Banks looked up at his homie and voiced his opinion.

"Pussy will have you doing things you normally wouldn't do."

Chase nodded at his right hand in silence as a couple of seconds passed and he snapped out of the short trance and gave everybody a handshake.

"Look, I might end up laying up with shorty. I will hit y'all up to let y'all know what's up."

"Okay cool Chase, yeah let us know," everyone announced.

Chase stepped into his Caddy then proceeded to Shannon's crib.

Chapter 8

Chase drove up Walnut Street until he came to 57th Street and made a right. Continuing straight for two blocks he crossed Market Street. Crossing two more blocks he came upon Vine Street and made a left. With the Septa depot to his right he made a right on 58th Street and made left on Callowhill Street. Once he spotted a papi store on his right he knew he was in the right area. He made another right and found a parking spot in the middle of the block. After he parallel parked he cut off the engine and pulled out his cell. Shannon's cell rung five times then went to her voicemail.

"Don't tell me this bitch fell asleep," Chase blurted out getting agitated.

He called her phone once again same conclusion. Chase breathed deeply and exhaled contemplating his next move. He couldn't remember her house since the times he did stop pass he was high out of his mind. He then remembered it was always at night since she lived with her dad and he worked an overnight job. Snapping back into reality he called again then she answered.

"Hello," Shannon said in a groggy state.

"Yo wake the fuck up. I'm out front."

"Okay, let me throw something on. Be out in a minute."

Chase observed a light in a master bedroom turn on. Being that it was late he knew that was the house. He pulled out his knot and separated half his money and turned his cell phone off then placed both in the middle compartment. Chase sat back looking to his left until he spotted Shannon come to the door. Once it was clear for him to come in he grabbed the food, homemade iced teas, and the rest of the things he bought for the night. Once out of his vehicle he was about to cross over the street but was stopped in his tracks by a vehicle that refused to stop at the stop sign. Distracted by the car he didn't notice four males ducking in between cars creeping upon him. As he reached the steps and was about to open the screen door Chase was snatched back from behind and placed in a choke hold. The grip alone made him drop everything in his possession as the male who had his neck in a vice grip gave out the first order.

"Lay ya bitch ass on the ground face first before we put a hot one in you."

Chase knew what it was so he just followed what the man said. A second man spoke and followed up with a sharp kick to the right side of Chase's midsection. A sharp pain coursed its way through Chase's body as he inhaled deeply to embrace was about to happen next as one other boys spoke up.

"Look, fuck all that talking. Fuck that nigga up and go in his pockets. Matter of fact take everything you find on him."

After he spoke a hail of punches and kick begin to land on Chase's 150-pound frame. Being rolled on every which way he managed to block his face from receiving any damages. During the strong arm Shannon, who went back upstairs, came back to see what was holding Chase up. She spotted him being pummeled by the four mysterious men.

"What the fuck? I'm calling the cops!" she yelled as she ran out the door.

The four men scattered, breaking off in twos. Shannon kneeled down to assist Chase Money in the house. The after effects of the thrashing he just received had Chase dazed.

"I know I'm gon' feel it tomorrow. I'm still a li'l on from drinking earlier. That's the only thing keeping me from feeling them punches."

"Where the fuck they come from?" Shannon asked.

"Who the fuck knows?" Chase said while he began to walk over to his car.

"Where you going Chase?"

"I'm going to get my phone. I got to hit my squad up to let them know what happened."

After rising off her couch Chase strolled out to his car and gripped his cell phone. Thirty seconds later he entered and sat back on the couch with Shannon sitting down to his left in silence.

"Don't do nothing crazy Chase," Shannon said, breaking her silence.

"Fuck you mean don't do nothing crazy? I'm just letting my nigga know what went down 'cause he tried to stop me from coming. Of course I didn't foresee it being

116

that I was blinded by the pussy. Look, don't worry 'bout me. Just roll some of that Loud up.

Shannon remained silent due to Chase's high level of aggression. Reaching inside the black plastic bag on the table in front of her she pulled out the vanilla Entourage, unraveled it, and replaced the guts with some of the finest green sticky. Chase called Banks who didn't answer the first time he called. He redialed then Banks answered.

"What's up Chase? The pussy was that bad? You done already?" Banks said as he answered.

"Naw bro, I got robbed."

Banks was silent on the other end the phone waiting for Chase to say sike and that he was joking but it didn't happen.

"Nigga stop joking."

"I'm not Banks. This real talk bro."

After Chase spoke he tapped his pockets then continued the conversation.

"Listen they took a couple of dollars off me, that all-chrome watch, and our first necklace with the two small G's on it."

"Not the first jawn. You know we vowed never to lose that to remind us how far we got."

"Yo Banks round up everybody you can get. We 'bout to go head hunting after I smoke this weed to calm down."

"Cool Chase, I'm on it. Say no more. We should be there no less than 15 minutes."

After Chase hung up Shannon rose up from the chair she was sitting in and began to rant.

"You not going nowhere. Let that shit go. Whoever done this probably just some haters. Money, necklace, and a watch is not worth dying over."

Shannon was an inch away from crying she was so emotional.

"Who said anything about dying? If you was paying attention I said we are going head hunting. I know them niggas is from around here so we gon' ride around until we find a group of niggas then give them some lead in their diet."

Shannon shook her head at Chase's demeanor.

"No nigga, I heard you but who's to say them niggas ain't gon' be strapped. They might be smart enough to know to strap up in case niggas come looking."

"Get the fuck outta here with your crazy scenarios. As a matter of fact light that loud up and shut up. You over talking about if them niggas was smart. If them niggas was smart they would've offed me while I was laying on that ground. Some niggas love for you to hand them some rope so they can hang themselves."

Shannon ignored Chase's last comment but followed his orders. After taking a couple of hits she passed him the weed in the midst of him pacing.

"I think you should relax before you have a nervous breakdown."

"Who the fuck are you? Dr. Ruth?" Chase responded swiftly.

Shannon countered his response with a burst of laughter. Chase instantly grew inquisitive.

"What the fuck is so funny?"

Shannon gained her composure then answered.

"Chase Dr. Ruth is that old wrinkled lady who's the sex doctor."

Chase gave her a long empty glare then spoke.

"Listen bear with me, I'm a little disorientated right now. How would you feel after four bitches hopped on ya ass?"

Shannon sat in silence before she got up and took over Chase personal space while he tried to enjoy his therapy.

"Look I don't know what I would do but what I do know right now you need to relax and let me take care of you."

Shannon began to unbuckle Chase's belt but was unsuccessful as he nudged away.

"I'm definitely not in the mood for that right now. All I need for you to do is chill and enjoy this weed with me."

Shannon plopped down in the chair and smacked her teeth ending her temper tantrum by flagging Chase. As a result of being turned down her whole aura switched from a 25-year-old to a teenager. Chase shook his head while staring over in her direction. He took a couple of totes, exhaled, and his phone rang. Chase glanced to see who it was then answered.

"About time. Where you at?"

"Listen it's just me and Paperboi. I couldn't get a hold of Stacks and Scrilla," Banks said on the other end.

"That's cool bro. Where you at?"

"Coming up Vine. Where she live at again?"

"Look come up to 59th and Callowhill by the Septa Depot."

"Aww shit," Banks said while switching the phone to his left ear to make a quick right on 60th Street.

"What's up?" Chase asked.

"Nothing I already crossed 59th I had to make a quick turn but we 'bout to pull up now."

"Okay cool, I will keep a look out for y'all."

Chase tapped the red button on his phone screen then turned to Shannon who had her thumb in her mouth and eyes sealed.

"Yo wake the fuck up. I know you was listening, trying to act like you was sleep."

"Nigga I wasn't in your conversation, I was nodding off," Shannon said defensively.

"Whatever. My niggas is 'bout to pull up I don't know if they coming in or not so put something on just in case they do."

Shannon rose up off the chair and went upstairs. Chase took the last puff of the Entourage and placed the roach inside the ashtray. Awaiting the arrival of Banks and

Paperboi two minutes later Shannon made her way back downstairs in a pair of gray sweats and a T-shirt that passed her knees.

"They didn't get here yet?"

Chase shot her a blank stare since he hated rhetorical questions. Shannon was baffled at his silent but deadly stare remaining non-respondent. Chase's phone rang, breaking the awkward moment that was arising.

"Y'all here?" Chase asked answering his phone on speaker.

"Yeah bro we found a spot on 59th Street by the depot."

Chase hung up then wandered towards the front door. Once Banks and Paperboi seen him emerge from the house they hopped out the vehicle they drove in. Coming to a median at the corner Banks and Paperboi embraced their homie in his time of need.

"You good bro?" Banks asked sincerely.

"Yeah man, just some bumps and bruises. I ain't really feel nothing from drinking earlier plus shorty rolled up some weed so I'm straight right now."

"Cool bro walk us through what happened," Banks continued as him and Paperboi stood attentive.

Chased inhaled intensely before uttering any words. After exhaling he began the story.

"I parked, hopped out, and was about to walk across the street over to shorty crib and all of a sudden niggas was on my ass."

Banks and Paperboi glanced at each other then Banks gave his opinion

"I think this was a setup unless niggas was just around and was scheming and knew who you were when they seen you park."

Banks' comment made a swirl of scenarios arise, as Paperboi stuck with Banks.

"I'm gon' go with my gut on this shit y'all. It could be a matter of both but I'm with what Banks mentioned first. This shit was a setup."

Chase's phone chimed, signaling he received a text. He took a glimpse and saw the message was from Streets.

"Yo Streets just sent me a video."

After Chase spoke he turned his phone on a 90-degree angle so they all could take a glimpse at the video. Chase tapped his screen for the video to play. At first glance Paperboi instantly snapped.

"See Chase, Banks was telling you back at the Chinese store not to come out now niggas got you on video getting stomped the fuck out and robbed!"

Paperboi drew his Glock 19 he had concealed on his hip and put one in the chamber.

"Niggas want war. I'm ready."

"Chill, chill," Banks said as him and Chase resumed watching the video.

The video then switched from the melee to five people, with four out of the five donning ski masks.

Chase chuckled at the fact that Rizz wasn't wearing one. Paperboi finally calmed down and went back to tuning in along with Chase and Banks as Rizz began to speak on the video.

"I just want to let the streets know it's frauds out here. We the Paperboyz. Yeah, y'all see the shirts. We keep it real. On the other hand them Gwap Gang faggots, well y'all see how they frauding catches up to them."

Rizz stopped talking then reached inside his pocket and pulled out the Gwap Gang chain.

"See what happens to frauds in the streets? They manhood gets snatched away along with jewels and shit. So all y'all Gwap Gang fans stop fucking with them fake niggas and come over to where the real niggas is at. Log on to Paperboyz.com. Fuck that fake shit."

The video ended and a bizarre silence came over three fifths of the squad. Chase mainly since he rarely reacted on sight. Banks and Paperboi spoke first on the situation. Paperboi blew out some unwanted breath then spoke.

"Yo I'm ready to go blast at all them niggas."

Banks feeding off of his energy followed up with his own choice of words.

"I feel you Paperboi 'cause they getting personal now. I wish I knew they moms' phone number. I would call all of them right and tell 'em look it's time for y'all to purchase that Black dress."

Chase chuckled at Banks then spoke.

"Y'all niggas is crazy. What y'all fail to realize is this is a checkers move and we only deal in chess moves. Let's roll out."

"But what about the bitch? At least go in there and smack the shit out of her. If you don't want to I will do it. I don't mind smacking a bitch for revenge."

Paperboi's comment made both Banks and Chase laugh. Chase stopped his peoples in his tracks from walking in the direction of Shannon's house.

"Naw Paperboi it's all good. I got to chalk this one up. Let that bitch breathe. What I would suggest though is we get rid of all them bitches linked to her from the night we gripped her and her squad from the motorcycle club. If Shannon rolling like that then them bitches is guilty by association."

Chapter 9

Six candles flickered on each side of the nightstand as Vanity lay on her back staring at her reflection in her ceiling mirrors. Admiring herself in an all red lace teddy from Victoria Secret stroked her ego but she still was missing one thing: a man's touch. No matter how many times her pocket rocket made her have orgasms she yearned for a real penis going in and out of her vaginal walls. Caressing her breasts made her nipples supple and perky as she began to moan. The first name that appeared in her mind was Bishop Williams due to the fact that he was her favorite. Not only did he pull her out of her personal hells, he made love to her as if they were an union. Nostalgia influenced her thoughts as she was taken back to when her body used to tremble and tears rolled down her eyes every time their souls connected through intercourse. As quickly as she reminisced a frown formed on her face because the last time they made love he dropped an atomic bomb that almost killed every emotion within her body. He told her he was a married man grieving from his wife and going through a transition he couldn't fathom at the moment. Vanity felt as if he just used her for sex at first but when he told her about what his wife was going through and how his soul was falling apart she forgave him.

Vanity rolled to her left side and reached on the nightstand and seized her cell phone. Scrolling through her phone she came upon Bishop's contact info. As soon as she glanced and was about to tap her screen to notify him she placed the phone by her right side and exhaled the anxiety that was quickly building. Thoughts quickly churned in her brain as she spoke aloud to herself.

"You've come too far to turn back now. If you want this man like you say you do make the move."

Inhaling acutely then exhaling, gaining her composure, she picked her phone back up and this time she held the button down to quicken the process. Her phone spoke back to her, asking her what her demands were. Vanity spoke into her speaker.

"Call Bishop Williams."

Her phone followed the prompt and dialed Bishop Williams. His phone ran five times and as soon as her impatience was about to make her hang up he answered in a groggy state.

"Hello," Bishop Williams answered then cleared his throat.

"Hey Bishop, sorry if I woke you," Vanity said seductively.

Bishop arose and sat on the left side of his bed wiping his eyes then let out a yawn.

"Vanity I see you still have my number."

Vanity let out a snicker as she lifted her left leg in the air still staring at her own reflection with her phone tucked under her left side cheek and chin.

"Bishop now why would I get rid of it? You are one man I can truly say is impossible to remove from my life no matter how frustrated I get of not having you in my life the way I want you to be."

Bishop exhaled before responding.

"Vanity if we must bring up the past at this moment like I told you the last time we had intercourse my spirit was broken because my wife was departing from cancer and that is the only reason why we connected. Now in the midst of us connecting that way I brought you closer to God and pulled you out of your mental hells. What more do you want from me at this time because I feel as if my job is done."

Vanity sat in silence digesting his difference of opinion.

"I don't feel like we're done Bishop. You need a companion in your life. How long has it been since you let a woman set your soul on fire?"

"To answer your question truthfully it has been a while but I thought you told me you were here to help my daughter."

"Okay you caught me red-handed Bishop. I can't have my cake and eat it too?"

"No you know my spirit won't allow me to partake in any of your schemes. You either come correct Vanity or don't come at all."

"Ooh strong wording Bishop, but just to let you know I'm coming full force just wait and watch.

Click. Vanity hung up on Bishop laughing wholeheartedly. After regaining her composure she reached over her nightstand and pulled out her pocket rocket, her flat detachable piece, and lube. She screwed the piece on top then poured the slippery liquid on her fingertips, placing them on her clitoris and gently fondling herself. Reaching full arousal she poured more lube this time on top of the pocket rocket then turned it on. Placing the head of the small buzzing machine on her clit and began moving it in a small circler motions. With every motion her moans grew as she anticipated the explosion within her vaginal walls. As the tip glided gently her clit became stiffer, reaching its peak and sending shockwaves through her body. After her sexual eruption she inhaled intensely followed by an exhale. Her eyes instantly grew heavier and heavier with every breath she took to regain her natural state as she placed the pink machinery on her left side and rolled over to her right and dozed off.

$$$$

Bishop Jackson sat on the edge of his bed after being awakened from Vanity's fantasies. He relieved himself and couldn't fall back asleep. Pondering on Vanity had his spirit in a bind. It would be a lie for him to say he still wasn't attracted to her because his thoughts took him back to what she was wearing when she popped up at his office. His thoughts began to overthrow his mind as he lay on his left side. He began to breathe deeply to try and contest the feeling but it was too late. He instantly thought about if that knock never came at the door and saved him from the sexual grip she wanted to place upon him. Bishop was a prisoner of his mind trapped in the thought of her oral skills. He knew if he would've sampled that again he would be drawn to her like a bee to pollen. He pictured himself caressing her hair while she glided her tongue and lips on his rock hard manhood. After five minutes of ecstasy within his conscience he let out a grunt and squirted on the towel placed on his side. After releasing his testosterone he walked into his bathroom, wiped off his penis, and laid down to rest to get his mind, body, and soul in sync. One person that brought that balance was his daughter Erica, so he focused on the love of her while he drifted off.

Chapter 10

Knottie pulled up on 56th and Addison and made a right turn, driving down a few feet and parking. Hopping out of his black on black 750 Beemer he observed his surroundings to make sure not a mere soul was in his presence as he made his way to open his trunk space. After popping his trunk he clutched the night's earnings from The Happy Inn, closed the trunk, then began strolling in to middle of the block until he came upon a green door. Balling his hand into a fist he conducted a special knock resembling a beat on the door. Five seconds later a 6-foot individual with dreads opened the door and greeted his boss.

"Wah gwan boss man?"

Knottie nodded his head as he entered.

"Everything Criss. Everybody eat a food," Knottie said in his finest Patois.

His operative, excited from his boss's response, countered.

"You right 'bout dat boss man. It's 'bout da coil in unda mi mattress. Pussy Po-Po can't find dat rude boy."

Both men bumped fists then Knottie departed, making his way downstairs where all his work was being bagged up to distribute. The smell of the high grade marijuana was so intense you could breathe in the vapors and catch contact. Knottie placed the bag of money down and got the attention of his loyal workers.

"Listen up mi yout and family. King pass me the throne, so mi da top bad man now, see?"

Everybody stuck up their fists acknowledging Knottie's display of power. As he finished his cell phone began to ring. He took a quick glance ignoring the call since it was Simone. After a night of dancing and drinking she always wanted sex but at the time he was making his rounds collecting his money. One of Knottie's young top shottas approached him while he was placing his phone back into his pocket.

"Boss man Knottie, back at di club ya rude gal was dancing with some pussy clot. Me wanted to put a hot one in him but it would hurt business, see? So me and the dreads backed off."

"Mi no worry. Mi top bad man. Nobody take food from us, see? Everybody eat a food now cause of me."

Knottie's little soldier just nodded and stood by him as Knottie placed his hand on his shoulder signaling him to stay put as his phone chimed. Dollar signs flashed across his screen then Knottie gave out his mission for the night.

"Li'l Max time to grow big balls mi yout. Go pick up da green. Bring back the boss man duffle full of green."

Li'l Max nodded then proceeded up the basement stairs to exit. Once he came upon the tall doorman they bumped fists before walking out. The late night draft in the air caused him to place his hoodie on top of his head as he walked up the block to his black Buick Century. Once he made it to 56th Street he made a left, pacing a few feet in front of him was his vehicle. He stepped off the pavement but glanced up the street at a vehicle that had stopped at the stop sign a block ahead of him. He ignored the vehicle stepping out to get in the driver's side but didn't notice the car speeding up as he tried to place his key in the door. The car struck him and he rose off his feet and landed on the hood with blood trickling from his mouth, killing him slowly.

Chapter 11

Snap, snap! The camera of the CSI photographer sounded while taking pictures of Li'l Max laid out on the hood of his Buick Century. Three squad cars were on the scene as their police lights lit up the whole block. Spectators were sprawled around the area. Some stood on their porches observing what took place on their block. Detective Patterson pulled up and hopped out his vehicle with a coffee in his right hand, taking a quick sip. Stopping alongside the photographer he sighed at the sight of Li'l Max then spoke.

"Another dread. So what are they calling this one?"

The photographer took a step back to get two more pictures then responded to Detective Patterson.

"Vehicular homicide. Blood coming from the mouth signaling internal organ damage from the collision. Also from the way he was found I'm guessing the impact from the car made him land this way."

Detective Patterson observed while listening as he took another sip of coffee.

"Any witnesses?" he asked responsively.

"Just the usual old lady who called after she was awakened from the racket."

"Right, she didn't see anything. She just heard and made the call. I got it."

After the brief conversation Detective Patterson reached inside his left jacket pocket pulled out his mini flashlight and begin searching for clues around the premises.

"Well, well, look at what we got here," Detective Patterson said, stumbling upon Li'l Max's car keys.

"Can someone get me a pair of gloves?" Detective Patterson asked.

After his order was fulfilled he kneeled and picked up the keys. Closely examining the keys he came across one displaying the Jamaican flag and the words "The Posse" in the middle. Seeing that he knew the next move was to search the vehicle. He walked over to the passenger's side and opened the door, removing small fragments of glass before sitting down. He took a chance by pulling the glove compartment to see if it was open but it was locked. He then glanced at the keys as he found a small key that looked like it was a perfect fit after sizing up the hole. The key fit like a charm as he unlocked it, spotting a Mac 10 along with two cartridges.

"Someone come bag this up for evidence," Detective Patterson said while holding it up in the air.

A 200-pound man named Norman with navy blue PPD issued overalls walked up and collected the evidence.

"Now let's check to see what we can find in the trunk," Detective Patterson mentioned as he walked to the rear of the Century.

He placed the key inside the hole, opened the trunk, and found seven pounds of high graded marijuana.

"This one is for the books boys. Collect this so it can be processed and it is imperative that you note it's connected to my case. My job is done. Clean up and let's move out," Detective Patterson said while walking back to his car and driving around the corner to district headquarters.

$$$$

Knottie grew more agitated every second pondering on the whereabouts of his young shotta. He took deep tokes of his tightly rolled high grade Kush to dead any harsh realities building in his conscience. Two scenarios replayed in his mind, controlling his feelings; either Li'l Max got robbed and killed or the cops pulled him over and he's in cuffs. His conscience wouldn't allow him to sit still so he placed the half smoking Blunt in the ashtray and walked out of his basement office, trotting up the stairs.

"Mi finna go find Li'l Max. Hold it down," Knottie stated to his new doorman.

As he stepped out he spotted the cops' lights at the top of the block and decided step back in. Once inside he pulled out his cell phone and called Li'l Max while his doorman stood ground. Li'l Max's phone went straight to voicemail as panic began to sink in. One thing for certain Knottie knew how to think on his feet even when pressure was applied to the point it could bust pipes and create chaos.

"Jamar see what po-po doing up da block."

The tall lanky dread put on his hoodie that had the words "The Posse" across the chest then grabbed the .45 ACP that was on the side of chair he was sitting in. After concealing the shiny weaponry Knottie stopped him before he made it out to spectate.

"No ammo. Just see what's what."

Jamar nodded and handed him the semi-automatic weapon then he stepped outside, surveying in the direction of the cop lights. He made a swift left walking up a half a block in less than a minute. As he got to the corner he spotted the coroner lifting Li'l Max and placing him in a body bag. After seeing his brethren being zipped up he began walking back down to the house dreading the outcome once he told Knottie the news. Jamar knocked and Knottie greeted him instantly after the bang in anticipation. Jamar stood in silence until Knottie read his body language and addressed him.

"So what happened?"

Jamar took a deep breath then answered.

"Li'l Max go meet his maker."

"What?" Knottie yelled as he plopped down in the lookout chair.

Anger arose as he got up and walked back and forth in the small space between him Jamar and the front door. Picking up the .45 ACP in the same motion he rose from the chair, he cocked back the hammer then spoke.

"Eye for an eye, see? I know who hit us! We gon' show him who the real bad man is 'round these parts."

Jamar stood by as his boss ranted about losing one of his best soldiers. He nodded in agreement as he mentally prepared himself for war.

Chapter 12

Detective Patterson popped up quickly. What he thought was going to be a brief nap turned out to be three hours of nodding off. Waking up so suddenly had his adrenaline flowing as he checked his cell phone to specify the exact time.

"Shit 6 a.m.," he blurted out placing his phone in his pocket.

Detective Patterson arose from the chair then wiped the corners of his mouth and rubbed his eyes to remove any signs of sleep. Luckily he picked the right interrogation room as no one disturbed him for three hours. Unlocking the door and peeking, he crept out and walked amongst the other officers who appeared to be busy in the a.m. His first destination was the coffee and donut table then his desk area to busy himself on his case. Five minutes after grabbing two powdered donuts and freshly brewed coffee he arrived at his desk. To his surprise Detective Richmond was there working on her case.

"What are you doing here so early partner?"

Before she answered she twisted her face up and shot him an evil glare.

"Please don't remind me how early it is. Morello texted me to be here 'cause the reports on my bodies were due in today and he told me to be here bright and early."

Detective Patterson chuckled at his partner's complaint of reporting for duty so early. After taking a bite

142

from one of his donuts then sipping some coffee he responded.

"I remember those days with autopsy reports. Just to give you a heads up he's going to hand them to you while briefing you. He just wanted you here early because he's ambitious like that when he wants to tackle and solve a case in a timely fashion."

Detective Richmond shook her head then responded.

"So if he's this thorough why are you so gung ho on his movements?"

Detective Patterson's face wrinkled up at his partner's accusations. Detective Richmond was tickled by his facial expression as she responded before he could.

"That was a rhetorical question but I am still a little confused."

Detective Patterson killed her curiosity.

"Let me answer your question to the best of my ability so you won't be confused. I want to know just as much as you why was he's so comfortable talking to one of the most notorious mobsters in the city. Secondly IA hasn't even interviewed us yet. They only interrogated the captain and Freeman. I'm thinking that either they are incredibly smart or incredibly stupid. It's either or. Can't be both."

Detective Richmond always found her partner amusing.

"Listen, I'm sorry I even asked but you are too funny. Let me lay something heavy on you this morning good brother about conspiracy. Worst part about them is being consumed by them, and once that happens you to start to become one yourself."

Detective Patterson smiled at his partner.

"Looks like someone has been reading lately. Where did you get that from?" he asked sarcastically.

Detective Richmond gave her partner a love tap on his right left arm then answered.

"Ha-ha smart ass. To answer your question I was reading one of Bishop Williams' books. It mentioned something about your mind's energy and how powerful our thoughts are. Basically to break it down in simpler terms what you focus on mostly is what you become in the physical."

A slight pause came in between them as Detective Patterson digested his lesson for the day.

"Oh okay. That's deep. I can dig it."

Detective Richmond shot her partner a grin then continued the conversation.

"Now onto you. I heard you caught another body last night on your case. Do you think they are related?"

"I don't know what's going on in them streets but whatever's brewing it's starting to get crazy. This boy couldn't have been older than 25. Mac 10 in the glove compartment, seven pounds of marijuana in his trunk."

After hearing that Detective Richmond grew even more inquisitive.

"So what was it an attempted robbery?"

"Vehicular homicide," Detective Patterson said, sounding out every syllable then continuing. "Here's the kicker. I found his keys and guess who I found out he's connected with."

"Who?" Detective Richmond leaned in as she grew eager to hear his answer.

"The Posse," Detective Patterson answered.

Detective Richmond went back to her regular posture before being enthused by her partner's statement.

"So what's your plans on cracking this case?"

Detective Patterson paused at his partner's inquiry then answered.

"I think I'm going to move off of what I learned about the guy they call Knottie. He shouldn't be on the streets and what I found in that trunk lets me know he know he's connected somehow. Remember the bar owner Barrington and how he explained this character. It's like he's younger version of King."

"Okay Columbo. I'm behind you on that but you know when you start at the top shit starts to trickle down."

Detective Patterson laughed at his partner's description of his detective duties.

"Now I know that's not from Bishop so where did you get that philosophy from?"

"That was from my dad," Detective Richmond replied while chuckling.

The laughter between them was interrupted by Captain Morello entering their space.

"I'm glad to see yous two are in good spirits. My office pronto."

Both detectives glanced at each other with bewilderment written on their faces. It was like walking in a tunnel without a flashlight entering his office surprisingly.

"Ladies first," Detective Patterson said jokingly as they strode in the direction of his office.

Both detectives entered Captain Morello's office three steps behind him and remained standing out of respect awaiting him to state they could sit. But this particular time he left them standing as he went inside his desk and pulled out an envelope placing it on top of his desk.

"First thing first. Richmond here's the autopsy reports on both victims. They were strangled but semen was found in their vaginal walls. We don't know if it's the perpetrator's or who it belongs to. Our job is not to speculate as you already know. It's our job to close cases."

Detective Richmond nodded in agreement and remained silent.

"You know what I need from you Richmond. I expect you to go above and beyond your call of duty. This case might get a little tricky due to the circumstances but I know you can handle it. Hopefully we don't have a serial rapist/killer in my district. That's the last thing I need running around in the 18th."

Captain Morello inhaled deeply and exhaled then focused on Detective Patterson. He began to look on top of his desk then under his desk.

"As I look around my area I can't seem to find any paperwork on last night's body."

Richmond chuckled at the Captain's comedic barb as he continued.

"I'm going to need that ASAP sir."

Captain Morello paused from swallowing then continued.

"Where are you with your case?"

"I—"

Before Detective Patterson could get a response out Captain Morello interrupted.

"I'm going to need you to focus on your business. What's going on in this precinct has been going on since it's been here. Leave the past in the past and let's move on to solving these cases. Now with that being said you two are dismissed. We will talk later on progress."

Chapter 13

Clad in an all-white bra and boy short set Erica posed with her ass in the air as she stared directly into the camera lens. Mr. Hard, who suggested the outfit, said she looked like she was auditioning for the Victoria's Secret Runway Show. While the photographer snapped away at all angles Mr. Hard was filming for his online reality segment, which was a part of his empire.

"That's it, that's it. Make love to the camera. I know the fans are going to love this introduction to my new chocolate bunny Silk-E. Anything you wanna say to your new fans?"

Erica remained silent and rose up from her knees and turned her back to Mr. Hard while switching. While cat walking in her all white stilettos she unsnapped her bra placing her left arm across her breasts and tossed her bra over her shoulder with her right hand.

"Wow! That's what I call the silent no look. Did you catch that Dexter? Mr. Hard asked the cameraman as he snapped away.

"Give us something for the road to take us home Silk-E," Mr. Hard instructed.

Silk-E turned around with her index fingers over nipples and widened her legs for her last pose.

"Wow, I know that's going to get a lot of fans riled up. That's a wrap," Mr. Hard said as he turned his video recorder off then congratulated Erica on a job well done.

"Bravo, bravo. You're going to gain a lot of fans from what I just shot."

Excited about the venture she took ten steps forward over into Mr. Hard's direction to discuss details.

"So Terrence Harden could you give me the full rundown on Go Hard Enterprises?"

"Sure, well it's no secret you already got your 10G bonus for signing on. Now the 30 minute special we just shot I'm going to edit then send out an alert to everybody that's subscribed to my website. It's up to 200K round about and on the average 50 thousand people respond when I introduce new talent. Every individual who wants to watch the video pays $1 so you do the math and remember you get 10% off of every video I post of you."

"Damn, so on top of the 10G bonus I can make $5,000 for the half hour video?"

"Yes. Now let me tell you about a certain scenario. Salene, my girl from London, and Corine from Brazil tag teamed on one video and did a girl on girl scene. It included kissing, oral, then sex toys. Only 50 thousand people watched it but they subscribed over five times to view it. The video made 250 grand in two weeks."

"So people actually pay to watch stuff like that?" Erica asked inquisitively.

"You'd be surprised at what people pay to watch over the internet. That's why I'm cashing out. So now that you know the ins and outs get some ideas on what how you want to showcase yourself to your fans."

A nervous spell shot through Erica's whole body as a million thoughts swirled through her brain. Her stomach did like 20 flips as she felt like she was about to shit bricks. Mr. Hard read her facial expressions and counteracted.

"Look don't be all nervous. It's not like you have to do it tomorrow. You got a couple days."

Terrance's words uplifted the worry spell as Erica felt like she could breathe again.

"Thanks Terrance. I was about to say. Now I'm not shy or anything but a bitch needs some time to try and top what Salene and Corine performed. We can discuss that later. Let me go get dressed," Erica said as she began to walk in the direction of the dressing room.

After entering the room she began putting on her bra then jeans as her phone began to ring. A huge grin formed on her face once she noticed who was calling.

"Hi Daddy," she answered ecstatically.

"I just wanted to talk to my favorite woman in the world."

Bishop Williams' words soothed his daughter's soul as she always enjoyed hearing him acknowledge her with those terms.

"Aww thanks Daddy. I appreciate the gesture. How are my two favorite men in the world? I hope one is not being a brat."

"You know me. I'm at one with myself and DJ he's fine. All he needed was to be around some significant male figures."

Hearing her father bring up male figures caused a little frustration to settle as she exhaled then spoke.

"Speaking of male figures, how's his father coming along?"

"A whole lot better than when you were here. He's on the right track. I even have him reading some of my books."

"I'm impressed Daddy. I appreciate that. DJ needs his father."

A brief silence interrupted the conversation as Bishop was in transition with the two main reasons of why he was calling. He took a breath then proceeded.

"You're welcome Erica. I'm only doing what I'm supposed to be doing. Now look, now that we got that out of the way there are two things I want to discuss with you. Let me get to the bad news first. You remember Darnice? Her daughter Deseree was found dead a couple of days ago."

"Oh my God. Dad are you serious? We danced at the same club."

"Well I read about it in the paper along with some other girl named Chanel Cunningham a.k.a. CC."

"Oh my God, CC was my girl. Even though we went through our little problem due to Dawud crazy ass we became cool. I'm glad I got away from that crazy place. Somebody killing strippers now."

"Well that's not my job to find that out. I was just passing on the news to you. Now second order of business, there's someone who wants to meet you to do some work with their non-profit business. She's familiar with your work and would like for you to be a spokesperson. It's a non-profit that deals with young females who want to indulge in the fast life. The name is of this business is Your Guide to Wings Organization."

"Well give her my number. I will see what we can put together. Anybody you conduct business with I feel like I can already trust them."

"Thanks Erica. Now hopefully this move will make you turn over a new leaf in life."

"Dad I would like this conversation to end the same way it started. I'm about to start making more money than before having to do less. As matter of fact I will start sending money so you can put it in my savings. I'm planning on moving when I return. Now look, I have to go I have an important meeting soon. Let me know when the funeral is going to be so I can make plans on being there."

Bishop sighed then responded.

"Okay, I sure will 'cause me and DJ miss you dearly."

"Okay, Dad, I'm hanging up. I love you. Kiss DJ for me."

"Okay, Erica. I love you too."

Chapter 14

Frank and Maria tongue wrestled while their bodies interlocked in the missionary position. With every stroke she moaned and gripped his lower back, pulling him closer until their pelvis muscles intertwined.

"Deeper Frank deeper!" she instructed between her heavy wails.

Her legs began to tremble as her walls became tighter and her grip on his lower back and buttocks weakened. Frank's breathing became heavier after her orgasm as he collapsed on her chest then rolled on his side sweating profusely.

"Not bad for a half dead man."

Frank chuckled in the midst of catching his breath.

"Only your crazy ass would say something like that after I made you quiver like that."

"Whatever Frank I thank you for the orgasm but don't think you're falling back into my good graces since you made me cum."

Frank exhaled, trying to remain calm and not become quickly enraged.

"Listen I'm not gon' entertain your bullshit right now. I'm feeling good and you're not going to kill this vibe."

"Oh God please. What vibe?" Maria asked disgustingly.

His comment made her rise as she directed herself to the bathroom for a bird bath. Ten minutes later arriving with her head and body fully wrapped in towels Frank stared and recognized his wife's beauty and commented.

"You know I still remember the first time you spent the night at my house. You came out looking the same way."

Maria denied him of trying to sucker her into his smooth talk.

"Please Frank save the reminiscing for some other bitch that wants to hear it," Maria said as she was about to enter the walk-in closet.

Frank shot his wife a glare after she killed his smooth pimp vibes.

"Okay now you're pissing me off with the sarcasm," Frank said, raising his voice as he followed her into the walk-in closet.

Maria pulled the light string in the middle of the closet and began to peruse through her blouses. With every blouse she moved Frank noticed her mood changing and she was on the verge of exploding. He began a countdown in his mind similar to when NASA was conducting a space shuttle lift off.

T Minus 5, 4, 3, 2, 1.

Right when he approached lift off status she turned around and detonated.

"You know what Frank I just don't know who you are any more. I mean what the fuck. You were a cop and made rank with sergeant. Now you're a wannabe gangster. What the fuck?!"

Frank stood inside the closet with a blank stare as he didn't know how to respond. He was smart enough to know to remain silent because once she reached this level he was on the verge of being shot or stabbed. He watched her walk into the back corner of the closet and move her pants then pulled out his first uniform he wore as a sergeant from his 18th District days. Frank's eyes lit up like a kid on Christmas receiving his favorite gift. With tears streaming down her face she handed him the uniform.

"See this? This is the Frank I know and fell in love with."

After displaying her emotions she plastered her face on his left shoulder and wept.

Frank caressed her back with his left arm while holding the uniform in is right. Staring at the uniform Maria was oblivious to the fact that pulling out this uniform put a whole other plan into motion.

Chapter 15

The entire Gwap Gang was in attendance at Scrilla and Paperboi's crib on 54th and Chestnut due to Chase Money and Banks calling an early but necessary meeting. The reason being was due to the incident that transpired with Chase and how they needed to reform the movement and be cautious within the streets. The 42-inch plasma flat screen in the living room displayed the latest Streets DVD. The video of Chase being robbed and stomped didn't make the cut as Streets told them he wasn't gon' burn any bridges with them but it was circulating on social media and small blogs. It was spreading like a wild fire in California. The Gwap Gang was even being questioned by their fans about why they weren't responding. As a result of not being responsive they were losing subscriptions from GwapGang.com. Taking tokes from the weed that was circulating in the room Banks stood up and paused the DVD to release and voice his frustrations.

"I just want to start off by saying I don't believe we are losing fans behind this shit. I'm truly not feeling the fact that niggas is taking food off my plate." Everybody remained silent but attentive while letting him vent. "These fuck niggas trying to take what we built. I'm not trying to hear that and I'm not gon' stand by and take the peaceful route either. I say we go see them niggas on some real street shit since we know what we are capable of doing."

Paperboi spoke up presenting himself in agreement with Banks.

"Real rap. Banks is right. We built this Gwap Gang movement from the bottom on some untouchable type shit. We've come too far to let some crab in the barrel ass niggas bring our empire down. Chase I know you don't want us out here making mistakes putting everything in jeopardy but there comes a time when you got to defend your castle and that time has arrived bro."

Everyone sat in silence anticipating Chase's response staring over in his direction while he lay back in the leather recliner. After soaking in the feelings of his fellow soldiers he sat upright then addressed them.

"Both y'all right. We gon' go see them niggas tonight and put an end to this fake beef shit."

Everybody was still as they weren't expecting that type of response since his mannerism put him in a box to where he always chose money over violence. 99.9% of the time, no matter the situation, he chose the nonviolent route was but this was different for Chase. His back was against the wall and he was ready to come out guns blazing. Before he could utter another word a knock on the front door put a halt to the conversation as Scrilla answered the door.

"Oh shit, what this nigga doing out here?" Scrilla asked as his cousin Tyrik was the guilty culprit of interruption.

"What's up cuz?" Paperboi acknowledged his peoples as he entered.

"You know me man, getting to the money. What's good wit everybody? Y'all got some new shit out yet?" Tyrik asked while making his rounds around the room.

"Naw man, but best believe we working though," Scrilla answered.

"Look, it's been a long ride. Let me sit down for a few minutes then I will let y'all know why I'm popping up unexpectedly," Tyrik said while he plopped on the couch then jumped right back up like something caught a hold of his ass.

"What the fuck?!" Tyrik yelled.

Everyone surrounding was clueless as to why he made the sudden movement until Scrilla detected why from observing where he decided to sit.

"Oh shit cuz, my bad," Scrilla said while reaching under the pillows on to the couch.

"This is why nobody was sitting there," he continued as he pulled out the gang's heavy artillery.

"Damn, what y'all going to war wit Iraq?" Tyrik asked jokingly causing everybody to laugh on cue.

"Naw man, it ain't that deep but we stay prepared just in case we do have to cross that bridge," Scrilla said while showing off the heavy duty .44 mag Army edition.

"This thing right here is powerful. Me and Paperboi shot it in the park the other night and it took a chunk of bark off a tree so imagine what it can do to one of these fuck niggas out here."

After placing it back in its original place of concealment Tyrik and Scrilla transitioned from subjects and started to discuss his presence.

"So what's up cuz? What brings you out Philly?"

"I'm in search of some exotic or Kush. Either one would be good."

Scrilla's eyes illuminated at the sound of money.

"Shit, you came to the right place. Banks we still got them ten joints in stock, right?"

"Yup, how much he looking for?" Banks asked as he walked in the direction of the basement.

Tyrik contemplated the amount as he sat.

"How much y'all gon' charge me for all ten?"

Banks and Scrilla huddled by the basement stairs discussing the price while Chase un-paused the DVD and began to watch it with the rest of the gang including Tyrik. After deliberating Scrilla walked back into the living room area.

"How much you got on you cuz?"

"I got 20 on me. Is that enough?"

"Hell yeah, you can have the whole package for that," Banks yelled before making his way down in the basement to fulfill Tyrik's order.

Tyrik rose up and went out to his forest green Range Rover he arrived in then came back with knots of Benjamins. Once he arrived back in the house Banks handed him the duffle full of Kush. During the transaction Chase's cell begin to ring. Glancing at his screen he grabbed the remote and paused the DVD and told everybody to quiet down before he answered.

"Scarcetti, what's up?"

"Chase Money, my main man. Yous in for some good news today. Round up the gang and meet me at the office today."

Chase looked at his phone then put it back to his right side of his face.

"Why can't you just tell me over the phone right now and save me the trip?"

"Cause the news is too good to tell you over the phone, that's why. Look I'm not taking no for an answer so be here."

Scarcetti hung up after giving Chase Money his orders for today. As soon as Chase was about to turn the DVD back on his phone began to ring again. He glanced at the phone and exhaled in frustration as he sent it straight to his voicemail. The caller was determined to chat with Chase Money as they called him repeatedly. His reaction every time was to send them to voicemail. After the seventh time Chase was agitated and started browsing through his phone to put the caller on the block list. Paperboi distracted him by asking who the caller was.

"Yo who keep blowing ya phone up dog?"

"That bitch Shannon. I know she calling to gas me up with an apology. You know that cry in your ear so you can have sympathy type of bullshit. I ain't falling for it bro. Believe that."

Paperboi chuckled at Chase's analogy. Since he knew his homie like the back of his hand he knew it was all stubbornness and ego.

"Man just answer the phone. She gon' keep calling. Give her that much just to see what she got to say. If it's bullshit then give the bitch some rope and let her hang herself."

The rest of the squad laughed at Paperboi's exit strategy as Scrilla, who was on the sideline, responded.

"Yo Paperboi you crazy. Yeah Chase just answer bro. Ain't nothing wrong with hearing what she got to say."

Chase looked over the whole room at who was attendance thinking on the opinions given. His phone began ringing all over again as he answered.

"Yo Shannon, what's up?"

A brief pause came in between them after Chase answered. Shannon could be heard on the other end sobbing. Chase shook his head in disgust, took the phone away from his mouth then addressed his squad.

"I told y'all. She on the phone crying and shit. I should put her speaker," Chase whispered as he placed the phone back up to his right cheek.

Paperboi and Scrilla, awaiting him to put her on blast, tried their best to persuade him to go forth with putting her on speakerphone.

"Yeah dog put her on speaker," Scrilla said aloud.

Chase put his hand up then spoke into the receiver.

"Listen Shannon I don't got time for the fake sobbing and shit. What's up."

"I'm sorry Chase but they forced me to do it," Shannon replied through her whimpering. "I didn't want to have any part in it. Even my friends neglected me when I said no so it was like I was left with no choice but to go along with the scheme."

Not feeling any ounce of remorse since his heart was colder than Alaska at the moment Chase replied.

"Okay thanks for your apology but I can't fuck with you after that. You just showed me you a follower and you can't think for yourself. This the last conversation between us. Have a good life."

Chase hung up then focused all his energy on his squad.

"Listen, erase all them bitches we met out your phone from the night of the show at the motorcycle club."

First person to complain as usual was Scrilla.

"Aww man the shorty I gripped that night was the best head I ever witnessed."

His comment caused an uproar as Chase was the only one who didn't dignify his comedic expression.

"I'm serious. Her oral skills aren't important enough to catch a bullet for. Niggas is hungry and they gon' come at us from every angle since we on top. We got to stay on point 24/7."

Chase paused then continued.

"Just know that them niggas who set me up got everything coming to 'em. We gon' go see 'em. Ain't no doubt about that."

Chapter 16

Bishop Williams opened his front doors greeting three women and one man who were all sharply dressed in business suits. All in attendance were state reps interviewing him for the upcoming city councilman opening for the district. Bishop Williams found it an honor that he was sought out by the political powers that be so he didn't want to turn them down until he heard what was being offered. Once inside his office they were all seated and the process began. The first one to speak was one of the women, Clara Brown.

"So Bishop Williams let's get straight to the point. Our group has thought long and hard and we came to the conclusion that you would be the perfect candidate for City Council and we will back you 100%."

Bishop Williams smirked and nodded before responding.

"Politics. I mean why me? I know very little about politics."

"Well we based our decision off the work you accomplished in the community. You're a stand up man and we need more like you to represent for the city," Gerald Waters, the only male representing for the committee, said.

"I understand that but I'm a man of God and I feel like I would compromise that by having to change my way of thinking based on politics. I politic God's way, not by man."

"That's why we are here to let you know you're the perfect fit. We need more of God's people in office to clean this city up," Gerald Waters said while the women remained silent but nodded in agreement.

"Hold on. I thought I turned this off," Bishop said as his phone chimed.

He glanced at the screen, putting him on notice about the important meeting with five representatives. His whole demeanor changed as he noticed only four present.

"Okay, sorry for the slight interruption. I'm back. Now before we proceed I have an important question before we move on. Where's the fifth member that's supposed to be present?"

All four members sat in confusion, baffled at Bishop's questioning of the missing member as Gerald spoke up.

"I don't get the tone of your question? What does that have to do with anything? This is the foundation of the process. A missing member doesn't conflict with anything."

Bishop grew agitated that he danced around the question.

"It's not about the tone Gerald. I'm asking a legitimate question and I'm going to repeat the question because maybe you didn't hear me correctly. Where's the fifth member?"

All four members remained silent for a brief second then Clara spoke again.

"Sir no need to get hostile. The fifth member couldn't make it. He's out of town on other business."

"My sentiments exactly. I know somebody could've stood in for him to make this farce of a meeting look more legit. Plus since we started this meeting Clara and Gerald are the only ones that have spoken. I think this meeting is adjourned. But before you go could you please leave that gentleman's name?"

The state reps just got up and left his office without leaving a name, sensing Bishop was prying into their business. Bishop Williams shook his head at the sight of them leaving. His intuition led him to believe he wasn't picked by who was present but the man who was absent. He was relieved that before the scandal was set in motion he buried it. Bishop pulled out his laptop and decided to do some research of his own which he should've completed before agreeing to even meet with them. He Googled the five top state reps for Philadelphia as their images popped up. To his avail the four that were present in his office were there. Scrolling over he came upon the last and missing member of the committee. Everything was starting to sink in as his true enemy revealed himself. Everything was coming full circle for him and his remaining family. It was time to come clean about his past mistake for the sake of losing his daughter. He immediately picked up his cell to call Erica. His phone call went straight to her voicemail so he decided to leave a message.

"Erica it's your dad. Look, it's very important. Call me ASAP."

$$$$

Terrance and Erica stood outside of LAX while he rubbed his palms together in anticipation of meeting his favorite porn star. Leaning on his stretch limo he began to express how he felt about the situation.

"Wow, this one is for the books. I get to meet the one female I used to sneak and masturbate to," Terrance announced.

"Oh my God, must you be a perv? She's not here for your amusement. According to my father she's trying to get her non-profit off the ground and she's reaching out to me so please calm down."

"Okay so she's turned over a new leaf. That still don't mean I can't let her know I'm a fan of her previous work," Terrance replied as he displayed his pearly whites.

Erica shook her head at her associate's perversion. As she opened the door to step back into the limo she left him with a few choice words.

"Listen, you're like a dog with that pink thing hanging out. I'm going to enjoy me a glass of wine while we wait for her arrival."

Terrance burst into laughter at Erica's analogy while she closed the door.

"Hater!" Terrance yelled out.

His yelp came with no response.

Two minutes later Amaziah emerged from the sliding doors with two suitcases and a beautiful woman in tow. Terrance adjusted his collar licked the tips of his pinky fingers and glided them across his mustache and eyebrows. With every stride Vanity took towards Terrance his manhood grew in his pants as he watched her move with the grace of a model on the catwalk. She was donning a black floppy hat and matching from head to toe with a black tulip dress and two-inch Yves Saint Laurent heels. All the men in the vicinity stopped to catch a glimpse of Vanity as her heels clicked on the concrete, causing them to stop and stare even if it meant some getting cursed out by their spouses. Once face to face with Terrance she took off her Fendi shades with her left hand and held out her right to properly greet Terrance

"Hello. My name is Vanity Jackson."

Her seductive tone made Terrance fall under her spell instantly. As she finished introducing herself she went straight into the purse she was carrying and pulled out the ball of lip-gloss and began to glide the object across both lips and mashed them together. After bouncing back to reality Terrance replied.

"Nice to meet you. I'm Terrance Hard and I'm definitely a huge fan of your work."

Vanity blushed as Terrance opened the door for her and she climbed into the back seat of his luxury limo.

As she got comfortable Erica glared into her direction mesmerized by her beauty as Vanity reminded her of her mother. The comparison made her want to pursue the facts on how she met her father. Vanity was the first to speak, breaking the silence.

"First off I would like to say it's a pleasure to meet the daughter of the man who helped me in my time of need."

Erica grinned back at Vanity as she always enjoyed to hearing someone complementing her father's philanthropy.

"Thanks. Nice to meet you too," she replied

"I don't mean to interrupt but can I tell you how much I'm a fan of your work?" Terrance said. "What made…"

Before Terrance could finish Vanity scrunched her face up and began interrogating him.

"Let's cut the small talk. What do you do because I'm about my business. I could care less who's a fan of mine."

Erica, who was taking a sip of wine, almost choked at Vanity being so direct. Terrance raised his arms and began pleading his case.

"Sorry if I hit a soft spot. I was just trying to break the ice between us. I'm about my business too. I run my own XXX webcam empire."

Vanity bobbed her head twice then responded.

"Oh okay, doesn't sound bad. How's your empire structured?"

Eager to always answer questions about his business Terrance answered.

"So I have 50K fans. I record a video and they receive and email to buy/view it for 99 cents. Based on what's in the video I can get all 50K fans to download it at least once."

Vanity duplicated her response as she raised her brows then responded.

"So since you're such a huge fan and you run your own webcam business, let me ask how much to bring me out of retirement so we both can cash out."

Terrance's eyes lit up as he replied.

"What about your business with Erica?"

"Listen, I'm a chameleon. When I see an opportunity I can't pass up I take it. So with that being said don't worry about our business. I'm talking about us now so again, how much are you willing to pay?"

Terrance glanced over at Erica who turned, minding her own business looking out the window still sipping her wine. After the brief contemplation Terrance answered with numbers he quickly crunched up.

"50K up front and 50K on the back end. Since you're an underground legend I can sell this video for $9.99."

Vanity sat back and pondered on the deal that was placed on the table. A few seconds passed as she held out her hand and replied, "You've got a deal sir."

Chapter 17

Detective Richmond walked into Dawud's barbershop, Boss Cutz on Walnut Street between 52nd and 53rd. Upon entering on her left was a Korean nail salon then she walked up flight of stairs. At the top of the steps she stood in a hallway as she spotted end a room full of shampoo stations at the end. She entered the door where she noticed barber chairs and walked upon a tall Hershey dark man with a beard and 360-degree waves in his hair. He was very well groomed sporting Prada shoes, Rock and Republic Jeans, and an all-black T-shirt with Arabic lettering on the front that translated into "Allahu Akbar." Instantly assuming Detective Richmond was there for the salon he pointed in that direction.

"Salon doesn't open for another hour."

Detective Richmond lingered, knowing she was in the right place, but didn't know if he was the person she was in search of.

"I'm not here for the salon. I'm here to speak with Dawud," Detective Richmond said while displaying her badge.

"Oh okay, pleased to meet you Officer," Dawud said while he stopped sweeping and held his hand out for a friendly handshake.

Detective Richmond declined his greeting and continued to show her authority.

"That's Detective sir. Now are you Dawud?"

"Yes," Dawud answered while placing the broom on the wall then sitting in his barber chair.

"Okay now that we got the introduction out of the way let me show you a couple of pictures and you let me in on how well you know these females."

Detective Richmond removed the photos from the left inside pocket of her suit jacket then passed them to Dawud. He took a short glimpse of both then gave them back. He began stroking his beard as he spoke.

"They just a couple of jawns I used to smash here and there. I'm focused on my deen now, trying to get my life back on track and be a good father to my child. My question to you Detective is why are you bringing this to me?"

Detective Richmond disregarded his brashness and moved on to further questioning.

"Well when's the last time you came in contact with them?"

Dawud sat in silence and stared at Detective Richmond. Detective Richmond being the aggressive woman she was wasn't buying the slight memory loss.

"Look I don't have time for you to be making up shit. Quick as I ask I need you to spit it out," Detective Richmond instructed while snapping her fingers.

Dawud stood up aggressively and flagged Detective Richmond.

"Man look, I don't have time for this shit. My shop 'bout to open and I got to get this money Miss."

Detective Richmond disregarded his statement and walked towards him spinning him around and proceeded with handcuffing him.

"Oh yes you do. I'm taking you in for questioning and DNA. And you can dismiss all the slick talk Mister. I'm not the one for it. You will catch a hot one inside your barbershop."

While being handcuffed Dawud switched his tone.

"Aww c'mon Miss. No need for all this. Look, I will tell you all I know right here. No need to take me away from my money. Plus you don't have any probable cause."

Detective Richmond chuckled then commented.

"Listen it's too late to plead with me now. And I do have probable cause. You're on my list of being highly suspected of murdering Chanel and Deseree."

Dawud pleaded while trying to look back as she forced him through the door.

"Murder? You got to be kidding me. This some bullshit. I'm a peaceful brother that gets a lot of pussy and now I'm looking at two bodies?"

"Well Romeo you know what they say; your sins will catch up to you. Now let's go. Don't shuffle ya feet."

"You not even gon' read me my rights," Dawud pleaded while being thrust down the steps.

"Fuck ya rights," Detective Richmond interjected.

After escorting him downstairs as they exited a couple of his barbers were walking up to enter. As she was placing him in the backseat one ran up on the car. Detective Richmond swiftly grabbed her nine off her hip, aiming it directly at the male, stopping him in his tracks.

"Damn babe, it's like that? All I wanted to know was what's up with the boss and why he in cuffs."

"First off, I'm not your babe. Secondly, don't worry about it. If he gets released he can tell you about it. Now mind your business and go upstairs to cut hair."

Dawud yelled out to his workers from the backseat through the glass.

"Yo y'all hold it down. Insha'Allah I will be back. This right here is some false accusations.

Detective Richmond placed her nine back inside her holster and hopped in the burgundy Ford Crown Vic proceeding to the 18th District.

$$\$\$\$\$$$

Dawud sat in the interrogating room after being processed fingerprinted and swabbed for DNA. He began perspiring due to the anticipation of questioning that was soon to some. He wondered what type of information they already knew and had in their possession but knew it wouldn't suffice. Before she returned to the interrogation room Detective Richmond told Captain Morello she had a suspect in custody and he wanted to be present. Five minutes later they arrived in the room as Captain Morello locked the door behind them. He then stood on the wall folding his arms in the process and glared at Dawud while Detective Richmond sat down and turned the recorder on and the interrogation process began.

"What y'all trying to do, intimidate me? Let me just start off by saying the only one that can break me is Allah. I'm not confessing to anything 'cause I didn't commit any crimes. I fuck a lot of females. I guess this is my punishment from Allah to change."

Captain Morello chuckled as Detective Richmond spoke.

"Listen, all we want to know is what you know. Evidence and DNA is gon' determine the rest."

"Fuck your evidence," Dawud spat at Detective Richmond before giving her a hard glare.

Detective Richmond and Captain Morello just reproduced the same transparent glare back at him until a few seconds passed and he broke his peace.

"Okay look, the shorty Deseree I was over her house and we was drinking, smoking weed, just chilling at first about to watch a movie. I don't remember what we were going to watch but that's irrelevant. We didn't even get to the opening credits and she was all over me. I ended up smashing and it probably was raw 'cause I was intoxicated but I can't remember that either."

Detective Richmond placed her index on her temple paying attention to every detail he was giving as she remembered that's how the scene was when they arrived.

"Okay, move along to Chanel unless you want to give more details on the night with Deseree."

Dawud inhaled deeply then continued.

"I'm complete on the night with Deseree. I left after we was finished having sex. Now as far as Chanel I was smashing her too one night and her phone was constantly blowing up while we were in the middle of a session. We had our beef between us 'cause she knows my baby mom Erica and she found out I was smashing Deseree too. All I know is she told me that night she wanted us to be in a real relationship and she was willing to let go of this anonymous guy she was dating. She did mention that he gave off this vibe that he was capable of hurting her. I didn't pay her no mind because you can't turn a whore into a housewife. I bust my nut and got the hell out of there because I left my gun at home. He wasn't gon' get the drop on me."

"Okay, so this all happened in like within a three to five day span, correct?" Detective Richmond asked.

Dawud contemplated then answered.

"Yeah, that sounds about correct to me."

A knock on the door followed up after Dawud answered as both Detective Richmond and Captain Morello were pulled into the hallway by DNA specialist Alex Jefferies to go over the details he came across.

"So guys his DNA is all over the scene but no fingerprints on the neck. That's the key to the case that will solve both cases. Once we get a match on those prints then we crack this case."

Captain Morello glanced at his detective as she groaned and walked back into the interrogation room.

"Today's your lucky day Dawud. You're free to go."

Dawud stood up as his face glowed with pride.

"Listen, I don't believe in luck. I knew I was innocent the whole time.

Dawud walked out of the interrogation room to exit the precinct. Captain Morello came in after watching him leave as Detective Richmond sat on the edge of the table with her hands in her pocket.

"Any more suspects in mind?" Captain Morello asked.

Detective Richmond exhaled her frustrations then answered to her authority.

"Yeah now that you ask Captain, there is one more person. Let me go so I can take care of that."

Chapter 18

Detective Patterson pulled up on 14th and Arch at one of the federal buildings downtown. His detections led him to seek out Chris Wallace, Knottie's probation officer, once he read his rap sheet. No man that was caught with an illegal firearm that you use to fight in wars should be on the streets. Detective Patterson smelled corruption like it was his own scent and knew where to follow it. He also prepared himself to hear a whole sack of lies on how Knottie was walking the streets and never violated due to what was taking place in the streets. After entering, showing his badge to security, and taking his gun off his waist, he entered the elevator and pressed the button for the tenth floor. The elevator opened up and he got off and directed himself to the receptionist. Displaying his badge he noticed she wasn't even paying the badge any attention. She was all in his face. Due to her smiling Detective Patterson noticed the overbite within her mouth and disregarded any advances. Two of his pet peeves about women were their feet and teeth if they weren't straight then he didn't have any problem ignoring them. If it wasn't for his pickiness he would have already fed his ego. He decided to remain on course and be cordial at the same time.

"Hello Miss. I'm here to see Chris Wallace," Detective Patterson said while putting his badge away.

The receptionist stared into Detective Patterson's eyes as she fell under the spell of infatuation while responding.

"Okay sir, let me dial his extension," she said, still glaring into his face and mysteriously dialing Wallace's extension at the same time.

Ignoring her seductive glare Detective Patterson sat down and awaited the arrival of Chris Wallace. Five minutes later Wallace strolled up looking like an African-American Old Navy model donning a plaid button down tucked into pair of tan khakis. Topping the outfit off was a pair of Timberland boat shoes. In his hands were file folders and he switched them from his right to his left to greet Detective Patterson respectfully.

"Happy to make your acquaintance Officer."

Detective Patterson counteracted with a chuckle then replied, "That's Detective but I'd rather discuss that in privacy."

"Right this way Detective," Mr. Wallace uttered as he led the way to his office.

Entering his office Detective Patterson closed the door behind them and instantly pulled out Knottie's rap sheet and began conversing.

"Listen Mr. Wallace I'm going to get straight to the point. I'm here to inquire about the whereabouts of one of your parolees; the one who calls himself Knottie and runs a crew called The Posse."

A devilish grin formed on the face of Chris before replying.

"I see you're very diligent in your homework. But I must let you know that information is very expensive. Now how much are you willing to pay?"

Detective Patterson remained cordial and responded.

"Look, I expected this to go just how it's going. Now that you asked me that lets me know you can be easily paid off and falsify documents. I bet you didn't even check up on him to know two bodies were dropped over in the 18th District tied to him."

Chris shook his head and rose from his chair to address Detective Patterson.

"Detective Patterson I'm a smart man. When the powers that be give orders and their money is long enough to take you and your family out you succumb to the same hypocrisy. Now if you don't like what you're hearing take it up with the judge. I will gladly give you his number 'cause they don't pay enough for me to be legit anyway. As a matter of fact if you're not here on official business get the fuck out of my office."

Detective Patterson went from cordial to renegade in two seconds, lunging and going straight for his jugular.

"Listen you fake Harvard looking mothafucka', speak up or I will choke the shit out of you. Right now I got the power so speak or forever hold your peace."

Detective Patterson let his G.I. Joe kung fu grip go as Chris coughed, trying to regain his natural breathing state.

"Okay, okay! Listen, King notified me today to get rid of all his paperwork, erase his files, etc. King shipped him back to Kingston for dropping his nephew to sit up under King. King is about loyalty so once King caught whiff of him power tripping King displayed his level of power."

"So you mean to tell me Knottie is in the wind. Fuck!"

Detective Patterson left Chris Wallace's office after hearing the news. Upon grabbing his nine and leaving he pulled out his cell phone and contacted Captain Morello. There were two rings and Captain Morello answered.

"Tell me something good Patterson. Not in the mood for bad news."

Detective Patterson paused briefly pondering if he wanted to let his captain in on the news once he answered his phone in the manner he did.

"Captain I'm downtown and I just found out the suspect has been deported back to Kingston."

"Okay that's bad news. I thought I stated no more bad news. Listen Patterson, I'm going to ask you something and when I do answer it to the best of your ability. The evidence you seized, where is it?"

Detective Patterson was about to start his car as his heart wavered, skipping a few beats due to the severity of the question.

"Captain please tell me you're joking. The scene was bagged up by C.S.I. I put that in my report. Now what happened after that I'm clueless."

"Okay IA is really going to be on my ass now," Captain Morello said in between sighs. After the brief silence he placed in between him and Patterson he spoke again.

"Look, get with Richmond. She just left not too long ago and said she was going after another suspect since the first lead went sour."

"Okay Captain. Let me hang up and get with her."

Detective Patterson called his partner on her cell and she answered on the third ring.

"Partner what's up?"

"Just checking up on you. What's ya 10-4?"

Detective Richmond paused then spoke.

"Bear with me partner. In my quest to solve this case I came back to Benji's club to question him about any other possible leads he might know about. Come to find out his club has been shut down due to a raid last night. He's sitting down the Feds right now as I speak being processed for soliciting. I need to talk to him so meet me there. I'm on my way. It's the building on 6th and Spring Garden, 8th floor."

Chapter 19

Benji sat in Agent Corley's cubicle handcuffed while Agent Corley typed up his paperwork. Benji's mind was in a whirlwind while trying to keep his composure after what transpired. Agent Corley finalized his typing and turned to Benji to share the details.

"And you thought we were just there for a simple shootout. That's how we find our way in. We look for weakness and we find it and exploit it. It was just a matter of time until you folded."

Benji shook his head at Agent Corley's brazenness then replied.

"I'm still confused on where you're getting your information from Agent Corley. Just to let you know I'm going to beat these charges. Just watch."

A smile formed on Agent Corley's face resembling that of The Grinch then he responded.

"Oh really? You're the owner and you keep bringing up information. You forget we raided your club and caught females soliciting. Hey genius, you're going down. Trust and believe it will be you."

Benji hung his head low to the sound of the music beginning to play. With his last ounce of dignity his head rose confidently.

"The fat lady didn't sing yet Agent Corley."

Agent Corley scoffed while picking up the folder containing all the intel they collected.

"You see this folder and where you're sitting Benji. You must be going deaf 'cause that fat bitch is singing loud and clear."

Detective Richmond and Patterson strolled on the scene after Agent Corley tried for the last time to break Benji's spirit. After flashing their badges and announcing their presence Agent Corley even displayed to them how brash he was.

"C'mon detectives take them badges back to your district. You know those toys don't hold no power in this building."

Detective Richmond smacked her teeth before retorting.

"Listen Agent whatever your name is, we don't have time for that nonsense. We are here for Benji."

"And may I ask for what?"

Detective Patterson came to the aid of his comrade foreseeing Agent Corley and his partner having a tennis match of words.

"We need him for further questioning of two female corpses. I know your charges are important but our case is just as pertinent."

Agent Corley glanced in the direction of Benji duplicating the same evil grin he displayed earlier.

"You hear that Benji the Pimp? Soliciting and two homicides. Looks like your reign as the underworld king has been cut short. Detectives you have my permission to take him but make sure he returns."

$$$$

Detectives Patterson and Richmond escorted Benji to the interrogation room inside the federal offices. Benji was the first to sit down upon entering, placing his elbows on the table and folding his hands. Detective Patterson found comfort in placing his back and left foot on the wall while Detective Richmond sat directly across from Benji. A brief staring match ensued as Benji was the first to speak.

"All that staring detectives will not work. I don't know what y'all know or what y'all don't know. Frankly I don't even care what y'all think you know. I just want to let you two know I don't have anything to hide and whatever cause you have for calling this second meeting between us I'm innocent. I'm not one of them young punks out here looking to make no deals. I'm from the old school. My blood turns to ice when you try to force something that's false. Now try me if you think I'm bluffing."

After his opening speech Benji sat back, folded his arms, and mugged both detectives. Detective Patterson clapped before responding.

"Nice speech asshole. But that won't work with us. Actions speak louder than words player. Now we already know we met with you at your club but we need you to corroborate. So with that being said let's start from the beginning. How well do you know the victims?"

"I know them very well they worked at my club. I collected money from them every week. It was strictly professional."

Detective Richmond interjected after Benji answered.

"Yeah, yeah, save the bullshit for the rodeo. You fed us that load last time. I have reason to believe you were more than professional with these two. I'm guessing you kept it professional as long you could hold out, Ain't that right pimp?"

Benji snickered before responding.

"C'mon sharpshooter, I see through your tactic to try and get me all riled up. What's funny about your little comment is I haven't been called a pimp since the late 90s. That was my old profession. I don't place my ladies on no corner or websites. I get my money the legal way."

Detective Richmond scoffed at Benji.

"And that's why you're here. For soliciting in your clubs. Do me and my partner a favor Benji and just let the cat out of the bag. We are tired of the games. The ball is in your court and it's confession time."

Benji sighed then went into explanation.

"Okay detectives, here's my story. I was at a breaking point with a little charming snake by the name of Dawud. He was using my club and my girls for his personal pleasures not knowing these girls shared personal bonds with each other. He had them all enchanted thinking life was some sort of fairytale. His baby mom Erica caught on to his foul ways. The only two that didn't were CC and

Deseree. A couple of days ago I met Deseree at her house she was getting ready for company. I remember her rolling some weed up while we were talking about how she needed to leave him alone and focus on her money. We ended up arguing 'cause she's hardheaded when she wants to be and I was trying to persuade her not to let him come over. I went over to CC's house probably like a day after 'cause she wanted to discuss a rumor that was milling around all my clubs. Now when it comes to CC we had relations before I had her working in my clubs. But being that I know the game the way I know the game I groomed her into being one of the best dancers in the city. Last thing detectives; that soliciting charge is bullshit. These same old agents been trying to catch me since the 90s. That's why I ended that and switched up and made the hustle legal. I truly do think someone is conspiring and playing puppet master. The truth shall set me free. I'm just hoping the truth gets revealed."

After his confessional Detective Richmond's phone rang.

"It's Alex. He must have arrived," Detective Richmond said, addressing her partner.

"Listen Alex, come to the 8th floor. Ask for Agent Corley and he will escort you to the room we are occupying."

Detective Richmond hung up then directed her attention back to Benji.

"Just to let you in on a secret that was my favorite forensics guy Alex. We heard your words. Now we are going to see if they hold up. Do you want to step into the confessional booth again before he comes in?"

Benji shook his head, remaining silent.

"Well partner I think we are done here until we get those results back. I know what we are looking for to solve this case. Hopefully the evidence we collect gives us what we need."

$$$$

Detective Richmond drove in silence from the federal building after the interrogation and results ending up as another dead end for her trail of solving the case. Thinking that Benji was her man had her frustrated as she was at the end of her rope of suspects. While deep in thought her phone rang, instantly changing her mood.

"Hey Mr. Sexy," Detective Richmond said, answering her phone and stating a nickname she'd given to Omar.

"What's up babe? I hope I didn't catch you at a bad time. I wanted to know if you was down with a night cap. I'm talking champagne and roses in your bubble bath type shit."

His words resonated, causing her face to illuminate with joy.

"Sounds great. I'm down. Not to switch the subject so fast but I just wanted to ask you how's work been for the last few days?"

A brief silence came in between Omar and Detective Richmond before he answered.

"It's been hectic. My stupid ass boss has been lying to me the whole time. I never knew he was an ex pimp. Come to find out he had a couple of girls tricking and got caught up. I've been running around making moves to save the clubs. That's why I'm in need a serious stress reliever."

"Oh okay, well look, my boss is calling me so again that plan sounds wonderful. I can't wait to get off and you better deliver or it's going to be a problem."

Detective Richmond didn't give Omar a chance to get another word in before she switched lines to talk to Captain Morello.

"Hey Capt."

"Any luck on the second suspect?"

Detective Richmond let out a sigh before answering to her superior.

"You know what Captain, I'm not even going to lie. I thought we had our man. Once again evidence proved us wrong."

"Hey, don't be so down Richmond. Sometimes you have to take a step back and go over every detail more than once to see what's what. Gather all evidence and the words of your suspects and put them all in a pile and crack this case. You know as I sat in my office and think about this case in particular I learned over the years of my career these cases are cracked by one event that will bring everything to a head. Word to the wise, stay focused and be patient."

"Thanks Captain," Detective Richmond said before hanging up feeling renewed.

Chapter 20

Robert Scarcetti popped the top on the Moet bottle he gripped as the vapors escaped. Pouring for his two colleagues and secretary, the first of five bottles was empty as the Gwap Gang entered his conference room.

"Welcome guys. It's a celebration," Scarcetti bellowed as he popped the second bottle.

"I got five of the biggest bottles so don't worry; it's going to plenty to go around."

Chase Money and the rest of the gang were oblivious to what the celebration was for but they joined in on the festivities anyway. Scarcetti poured then distributed them all glasses and assembled everyone in attendance around the polished wooden table that was in the middle of the room. Once everybody was in place and he had everyone's attention he addressed the Gwap Gang.

"What did I tell you in front of that building Chase? I sent those boys packing."

Chase's brows puckered before retorting.

"You mean to tell me the case is terminated?"

"Yes it's over. I ate them fuckers alive today Chase. I ate them alive to the point where as the city didn't even want the case back. Not gon' lie; it took a bit of falsifying documents as far as licensees. I turned a couple of you guys into professional security but hey, within that I learned the city wasn't even after you guys. They were after some club owner. But what I do suggest as your lawyer is to stay out of trouble. You guys might be public enemy number one. Now that we got that out of the way let's toast to success."

Everyone raised their glasses then took a sip of bubbly. After the tasting Scarcetti pulled Chase away from the table into a corner of the room by a window that displayed the city's skyscrapers.

"Hell of a view, right Chase?"

Chase Money took a sip from the glass then answered.

"Yeah, definitely. So why are we separated at the moment?"

Scarcetti beamed at Chase then spoke.

"Look, I wanted to discuss some other details with you. Seeing that you're the undeclared leader of your entourage I feel like you're the only one I can trust to make this happen.

Chase's brows frowned up once again.

"Spit it out Scarcetti. You don't have to keep running around the bush. We both stand up men."

"Okay look, I'm not gon' charge you guys for the work me and my office completed on this case. I will call this a favor for a favor. I scratch your back, you scratch mine. I want to introduce you to Giovanni."

"Giovanni. Who's Giovanni?"

"Sorry Chase, I'm so enthusiastic right now. But Giovanni is my nephew who owns the diner Broad Street Diner between Ellsworth and Federal. He's looking to expand into a whole new world between rap and couple of other ventures that I will let him discuss with you. I'm just the facilitator of you two meeting."

Chase stared out the window and contemplated the offer.

"So what if I decline your offer and decide to just pay?"

Scarcetti laughed at Chase's rebuttal and placed his arm around his neck.

"Now why would want to do that when there's thousands upon thousands you can make? Look, I understand your position right now. You need time from what's taking place. I'll let him know you need a moment to think it over. Don't worry, there's no rush. Now let's go over here and finish celebrating."

Scarcetti and Chase rejoined the others back at the roundtable. While indulging in another glass Chase walked back over to the window and witnessed his first sunset at such a high altitude. After swallowing the last of his champagne he observed Banks and Scrilla about to refill another glass.

"Ayo! Last glass. We got to be on point for tonight."

Chapter 21

Frank assembled outside Dante and Luigi's Italian restaurant awaiting the emergence of Fat Frank, the pickup man for Tony Moretti. Same name but different in stature as Fat Frank stood at six feet and weighed 285 pounds— 125 more than Frank. Always the one to use his size to intimidate, Tony Moretti only used Fat Frank for pickups suggesting no one would even try and pinch a bag out of his hand even if they knew a million dollars was in the bag. To go with his giant stature he slightly resembled Lou Ferrigno, adding more to the myth that he was untouchable. On this particular night the only one crazy enough to even try to touch him was Frank since he was knew the pickup was for sports betting and underground gambling clubs Tony Moretti masterminded. Learning this route from eventually gaining Tony's trust to manage pickups with Fat Frankie, he remembered one day they transported 100 grand one night. Frank's hands started to itch thinking about how much was going to be in the bag tonight. Having already waited for over a half hour he began to grow impatient until he heard loud laughter getting closer to the front door. Fat Frank was having a brief comic session with one of the cooks walking him to the door. The restaurant closed early due on pick up days and the cook had to lock the door behind Fat Frank.

"Ahhh! Haaa! You're a funny guy," Fat Frank said while exiting.

Once Fat Frank was spotted outside and Frank heard the door close behind him he threw on his ski mask and grabbed his artillery. Frank then sprung out of his car, closing his door and quietly weaving in and out of parked cars, remaining inconspicuous until he was between Fat Frank's silver four-door Cadillac DTS. He then began rocking the car until he set the alarm off. At the sound of the alarm Fat Frank took every ounce of energy he had to run over to his vehicle to see what set it off. With no one in sight he perused the block to see if he could spot the perp. There was not a soul to be seen running away. Fat Frank disregarded the situation and silenced the alarm after pulling out his keys to open the driver side of his car. Once Frank heard keys he quietly maneuvered himself in position to get the drop on Fat Frank while he was more attentive to opening the door then being observant to his surroundings. Caught off guard, Fat Frank received two blows to the right side of his temple, causing him to lose his balance and fall on his left side. Squinting from the pain that shot through his cranium he remained on the ground trying to regain his 20/20.

"You muddafucka', whoever you are you're making a big mistake. You're lucky I can't fucking see you right now."

Frank chuckled at the sight of seeing the giant so helpless. It also stroked his ego that he was the first to take him down. It would be a great legend to tell his son if he would ever have one. While grabbing the bag full of money he noticed Fat Frank fidgeting around his ankle area and he remembered he always concealed a nickel plated .32 for back up just in case he had trouble taking a man out with his fists, which never happened until now. Frank struck him two more times, this time in his nasal cavity, instantly breaking it as Fat Frank began bleeding profusely.

"Yeah you fat fuck, you never saw this coming. You were going to shoot me. Get up!" Frank said while searching for the keys that dropped from his hand during the first set of pistol whips he dished out.

After spotting them he opened the driver side of the door and unlocked all the other doors in the process. Then he snatched Fat Frank by the collar and opened the back seat and threw him in.

"Time to take a ride Frankie," Frank said as he started the engine and sped off to his next destination.

Chapter 22

Captain Morello sat back in a brown plush leather recliner in his dad's basement sipping Prunier V.S.O.P, Vincenzo Morello's favorite cognac. Captain Morello turned on the massager as he and his father shot the breeze about current events.

"So how's the family?" Vincenzo asked being that he was very strict on old school rules on how a businessman keeps his household is balanced.

Captain Morello sipped his cognac then answered his father a in joking manner.

"You know Dad every time you ask that question when we talk I feel like I'm in an interrogation room."

He and his father shared a wholehearted chuckle as he continued.

"Now as far as everything I couldn't ask God for more. If I did I would feel like I was being ungrateful. Vincent Jr. is thinking about becoming a chef after he graduates and Vanessa she's into the whole modeling/social media queen phase. Now Maria she's still my favorite housewife/teacher in the world.

Vincent placed a Kodak smile on his father's face as he responded.

"Great. Reminds me of when your mother and I decided to just leave you as the only child. We wanted more but as years passed us by we just decided just to let you experience a father and mother's love for yourself."

Vincenzo took a sip of cognac, placed the glass back into the cup holder, then continued.

"Now on to business. I called you over to discuss my board meeting. Since I've moved up in the F.O.P. you know I get to hear everything milling around the water cooler, capisce?"

"Capisce Dad," Captain Morello said, taking another sip from his glass.

"Now listen carefully. Your district is under investigation along with numerous districts. What happened with Frank is small potatoes. It's pressure coming from every angle to actually rid the city of corrupt cops. Frank's situation just added more of a spotlight to it. Now I know IA has been milling around you since they think that the shit starts higher in ranks. Shit just makes me think now I'm really glad that I saved your ass from getting moved from the 3rd District before Moretti and his henchmen really got their claws into your skin deep."

Captain Morello sighed at the fact that his dad brought up the past.

"Please Dad, don't remind me of my past digressions. Since then I turned over a new leaf and rose in the ranks."

"Yes I know son. Let the past be the past. But you do know Frank wasn't the only bad seed running around in you precinct, right? But what's done in the dark shall come to the light. Who knows that better than my son?"

Captain Morello sat up in the recliner, sipped his cognac, then placed the glass back down.

"So you have any names for me Dad."

A huge grin formed on Vincenzo's face then he responded.

"Now who's interrogating who?"

A brief silence came in between the father and son duo and Vincenzo broke it by speaking up.

"I was joking son but of course I know who's who. It's up to you to pay attention and know all of your rotten apples."

Captain Morello shook his head at his father's response.

"You always liked to play hardball."

Vincenzo chuckled at his son's displacement.

"And look at how you turned out. I never once questioned your integrity as a man because I know how I raised you. Even when you were going through the fire from getting involved with Moretti and his men I never had a single doubt in my mind that you were going to fall from it 'cause like I was told by your grandfather and he was told etc., men are going to make mistakes no matter what but it's how you rise after making them."

Vincenzo sat up and swallowed the last of his cognac then continued.

"Son I'm about to be sixty. I'm actually ready to retire believe it or not, you know, reconnect with your mom, travel, enjoy all the fruits of my labor from over the course of time. Second reason I called you over things are about to change."

"Sounds great Pop—"

Captain Morello was interrupted by three hard knocks that came across the window on the basement door.

Bang, bang, bang! Three more came across once the door that wasn't answered in a timely manner. Vincenzo rose up and moved the blind to see who the culprit was knocking unannounced.

"C'mon in Tony. What's the occasion?"

Tony Moretti was slightly frenetic about being hit.

"First off pour me a stiff one then I can get to the details. Hey Vincent," Moretti said, entering.

Vincenzo poured him a glass of Prunier V.S.O.P. and passed it to Moretti. Tony devoured the double shot, wiped his mouth then, spoke on his presence.

"Listen I got hit today. Net worth of 100 grand. I've been slipping on having the guys you hired for me Vincenzo to make sure that things like this don't transpire but that's why I'm here to renew a contract. But I need standup men and sharpshooters. I feel like someone is trying a hostile takeover."

Vincenzo waved his hand at Tony Moretti while Captain Morello sat on the side ear hustling.

"Don't get bent all out of shape. Sounds like it was only a hit. Things like this happen when the participating party doesn't comply with the rules and procrastinates. I specifically told you in the beginning you miss payment you will have no men. But this is where the buck stops. The Feds and IA are all crawling around the city like fleas waiting for someone to reveal any dirt. It's time for you to hire you own muscle. Maybe once the smoke clears we can do business again but as of right now we are finished."

Tony Moretti looked over in Captain Morello's direction about to fix his lips to ask him if he could hire anyone for him. Vincenzo sensed it and intervened immediately.

"Don't even think about asking my son. Business has been expired between you two since ya guy turned on my son over those stolen precinct guns that almost cost him his job. Still 'til this day I think about the path my son would have taken if his dreams were taken away from him. But again let me repeat myself; our relationship is on ice until further notice."

Tony Moretti knew when it was time to a leave a person's presence before the wrong things were articulated. He held his tongue as he rose up and walked to the door he entered to exit. Before exiting he left the Morellos with a couple of words.

"Philadelphia will always be my city; remember that. Let any muddafucka' know if he's willing to take that from me I'm not going down without a fight."

Chapter 23

Two cars deep the Gwap Gang drove over to 62nd and Callowhill beginning their manhunt for the Paperboyz. Their search ended when they closed in on 59th Street and spotted them posted up by the papi store. Chase Money made a sharp left on Regent, a small block in between, and parked at the end of the block. After hopping out they assembled to plot, plan, and strategize. Banks clutched his .44 Magnum as Scrilla stuffed the mini pump in the right side of his jeans. The rest of the gang kept it simple, each carrying two Glock 19s, concealing one and keeping the other in their shooting hand. After the preparation Chase Money spoke up like a general putting his army in place.

"Scrilla, Banks, y'all coming wit me. We gon' take Haverford Ave. and come up 59th Street. Paperboi and Stacks y'all can walk back up to where we drove and take Callowhill and make that left. Since y'all walk is shorter wait for my call so we can hit them from both angles by surprise. Listen, put both of y'all phones on vibrate too as well. I want to catch these niggas to the point they shit in the boxers."

Everyone agreed, splitting up in the two groups. Chase Money, Banks, Scrilla cut the corner on Haverford Ave. as Stacks and Paperboi walked straight up Regent. Once Chase Money and everybody else in his group hit 59th Street he pulled out his cell to notify Paperboi that they were on the block coming up. Paperboi answered on the first vibrate he felt.

"Yo we on the block coming up. Where y'all at?" Chase asked.

"We on Callowhill in the cut staring right at 'em," Paperboi answered in a whisper.

"Cool ,wait for about one minute then walk up on their blindside 'cause they gon' spot us as we walk up first. If them niggas pull out just start dumping."

"Cool," Paperboi said before they hung up.

Chase Money, Banks, and Scrilla strolled up the block en route to the corner but were stopped in their tracks by a black Denali pulling up on the corner. A 300-pound individual slid out the passenger side with a red and black biker vest on, addressing The Paperboyz in an aggressive manner, pointing at all five members. Chase Money hesitated after recognizing the heavyset man but stuck to his agenda of why they were present. Rizz was the first one to spot three fifths of the Gwap Gang as they walked up.

"Speaking of them faggots here they go right here. I guess they out for blood now."

Chase disregarded Rizz's statement, counteracting.

"Fucking right. Y'all niggas and that bitch Shannon set me up."

Fats the head/owner of the Soul Riders Bike Club intervened.

"C'mon y'all, it's too much money out here for y'all to be beefing. I guarantee it's something petty. I pulled up at the right time 'cause y'all would be full of hollows and Chase Money and his squad would be getting low, maybe on the run. And guess what? Both of y'all money would stop coming in."

While Fats was schooling his youth Paperboi and Stacks made their way to the corner after spotting Chase Money and the rest of their team. As they walked up Fats peeped how Paperboi strolled on the scene with a slight limp.

"Damn young boy, what you got a pump in ya jeans? Rizz you lucky boy 'cause these niggas was about to have you and ya fam on that funeral line. But to keep it real with you since you my fam y'all going about this shit the wrong way. I get money with these Gwap Gang niggas. If you trying to get money like them holla at me but if you gon' be in the way I don't want no parts 'cause I'm about my money at the end of the day."

Fats paused then looked over in Chase's direction continuing.

"Chase I saw the video and I'm gon' keep it real; that shit was a whack move. Since I'm here I speak up for this nigga's stupidity."

Chase extended his hand to Fats then spoke.

"Sitting here listening to Fats, you right. It is petty. Back in the day they jumped me. Me and my man's ran a train on his sister. Now we against all odds ready to kill one another. I know I can be the bigger person and me and my squad gon' squash it right here so we can get back to being focused."

Chase turned around to walk away as the rest of the gang followed suit. Fats called out to Chase, stopping him in his tracks.

"Yo Chase stop past the club when you get time. I got a line on something heavy I think you would be interested in."

"Okay cool, no problem Fats. We will holla at you."

Chase and the Gwap Gang departed as Fats as walked back up the block towards Rizz and the Paperboyz. Hopping back in the passenger side of his Denali, he rolled down the window and motioned for Rizz to come closer.

"Listen, got some business for you to handle. Make sure you on point. I don't need no fuck ups."

"Cool Fats, I got you."

Fats rolled the window up and spoke to his driver as they departed from the block.

Chapter 24

After attending Deseree's funeral and repast Erica decided to find serenity by spending quality time with her father. Pulling up to his sanctuary she hopped out her rented black 300 C and entered. Memories began swirling as the incense that was burning throughout hallway sparked nostalgia. Her lips parted as she displayed her pearly whites from being so overwhelmed with joy as she was about to hug her father. As she reached the door to enter his office her state of being made her forget to knock first. Her entering unannounced startled Bishop Williams as he immediately closed his laptop.

"Sorry Dad, it's been a while," Erica apologized.

Since it was Erica, Bishop Williams disregarded the trespassing.

"Don't worry about it. I was caught off guard, that's all. Come give me hug."

Bishop rose up from his chair and walked around his desk to embrace his daughter. After the display of affection she sat down and Bishop remained standing as they transitioned into conversation.

"So how was your friend's service?" Bishop asked.

Without hesitation Erica spewed off the details.

"It was okay. Sad but definitely a humbling experience for me."

Bishop nodded then continued.

"Humbling for you because?"

214

Erica inhaled deeply taking her time to answer since she knew this could turn into a sermon. And how her emotions were twisted she was not in the mood.

"Humbling because I feel like it could've been me lying in that casket"

Bishop curled his brow then responded.

"Why are you comparing your life to hers?"

A brief silence crept in their space as Bishop intervened.

"Don't block your blessings 'cause you're wrapped up in your emotions."

"I'm not Dad. She was a close friend of mine. Our struggles were parallel and my heart is heavy at the moment."

"Oh okay, I understand. But let me say this; she made choices in her life that led up to this. What have I always taught you? With every action there is a consequence whether good or bad."

Erica sighed then responded.

"Dad please, not right now. All I need is consoling. Why must everything be a lesson? I get it, we all make bad choices or mistakes. All I was trying to say was that she didn't deserve to die the way she did."

Erica placed both hands over her face and began sobbing. Bishop Williams rubbed her back with his left hand and simultaneously leaned over towards his desk extending his right hand to grab some tissue. Bishop Williams exhaled as sadness began to grow within his soul. With Erica so emotional he knew this wasn't the right time but on the flip side he had to swallow his pride and spill the beans anyway.

"Erica we need to talk. I'll be right back, I'm going to relieve myself."

"Okay," Erica murmured before using the Kleenex to wipe her face and blow her nose.

Bishop Williams entered his restroom and stared into the mirror, mustering up the courage to tell his daughter the truth about what was transpiring.

"Father the truth has come to the light. Now give me the strength to make it right," Bishop uttered at his own reflection poetically.

After his brief prayer he turned on the faucet and cupped the cold water into his palms and splashed his face. He then reached for his towel, dried his face, and glared into the mirror one last time, taking a deep breath. Before stepping out he place the towel on the rack then cut the light off. He walked in on Erica behind his desk watching the video he previously was viewing when she waltzed in unexpectedly. The look she displayed when she raised her head let him know the time had arrived to explain everything. If her face was a weapon she would have been on trial for killing her father. The hope of mending Erica's heart at the moment came crashing down as he watched her grab the laptop and toss it across the room. The laptop made a loud crashing sound that didn't even startle Bishop as he cared more about how his daughter felt at the moment than some laptop he could replace easily.

"You've got a lot of explaining to do," Erica bellowed.

"Calm down Erica. I understand how this may look to you. You're right, I have a lot to explain to you. But first you have to calm down so you can hear me out."

"Don't tell me to calm down. I have a right to be upset. You told me that lady came to help me and now you have the video of us."

Erica sat down and began weeping. Bishop Williams attempted to step around the desk to console his daughter but she stopped him in his tracks.

"No, don't even come close to me right now. You can explain from where you stand."

Bishop took a deep breath and exhaled.

"Where do you want me to start?"

Erica remained silent and just stared him directly into his eyes while tears streamed down her face.

"Okay, I will go back so you can get a full understanding of how everything coincides today. Your mom—"

Erica interrupted him as soon as the words slipped off his tongue.

"Please don't bring my mom into this. May she rest in peace."

Bishop instantly became livid from her interrupting him.

"Look, do you want the story or not?!"

Fear struck Erica like never before since that was the first time her she witnessed her father so wound up.

She didn't even answer as she stared at him in silence again.

"Now before you rudely interrupted me I was saying you mother, may she rest in peace, was married to Vanity's brother. I'm not going to say his name but he's a politician. They met where she used to bartend down Old City at a lounge called Triple K. During their tumultuous relationship she met me while I was in the process of becoming what you see me as now. We instantly fell in love after I showed her another side of life from the darkness she lived in. She divorced him and from the looks of it he's been holding a vendetta against me ever since."

Erica reached for another Kleenex and wiped her face.

"So what else did she do at that club?"

Bishop attempted to disregard the question by asking her a question.

"What does that have to do with anything?"

Erica began sniffling as her emotions were at an all-time high.

"It has everything to do with what you're telling me plus I want to know."

"Rumor has it at this club she was a hostess that slept with men for money. She befriended Vanity who introduced her to her brother. Now when your mom became stricken with cancer I felt helpless and around that time is when Vanity was coming around more often but she had an ulterior motive. I guess she wanted to know what it was like to be changed so I helped her but in the midst of me reaching out we had sexual relations. When your mom passed away she wanted your mother's spot and I knew nobody of Vanity's caliber could replace your mother so I declined. I guess her and her brother are trying to sabotage my life and they found a way by getting to you. Now how, I don't know but recently she came by and we were reacquainted and she gave me this DVD."

Bishop walked around to the front section of his desk area, opened his drawer, then pulled out the DVD with Erica on the cover and gave it to her. Erica turned the DVD around and read the back.

"What's their last name Dad?"

Without hesitating Bishop Williams answered.

"Jackson."

Erica gasped for air as the truth resonated within her soul.

"Oh my God. So they're related to that director."

Erica placed the DVD down on the desk, rose up from the chair, and placed her whole head into his chest.

"I'm sorry Dad for being so disobedient. All this time you were trying to save me from the horrors my mom witnessed."

Bishop Williams nestled his daughter tightly and responded.

"You know I learned a lesson too. I should've never withheld the truth from you as to why I was telling you to quit living the way you were."

After speaking he pulled her away from his chest and stared her into her eyes then spoke.

"Keyword being were, right?"

Erica chuckled at her dad's sincerity then replied.

"Yes Dad, as of today you don't have to worry about me living that way."

Their tranquil moment came to a cease when Erica's phone rang. She pulled out her phone ,glanced at the screen, and answered.

"Hey Mocha baby, what's up?"

"Nothing much, just trying to see if you wanted to step out with me and have a couple of drinks. I'm still feeling a li'l funny after the funeral."

Erica sighed then spoke.

"Yeah girl, I feel you. I haven't been the same either. Where you trying to go?"

"Right now I don't know. Just come to my crib and we can figure it out from there," Mocha responded.

Erica's face curled up as she felt the urgency within her friend's voice.

"Is everything okay Mocha?"

The other end of the phone was so silent you could hear a pin drop. The quietness caused Erica to glance at her screen thinking the call dropped.

"Hello, Mocha?"

"My bad E. Girl I'm so jumpy right now. I smoked a whole L to my face and my nerves are still racing. Look,

I got a lot of information to share with you so mentally prepare yourself before you get here."

"Okay, I'm on my way," Erica said as she hung up.

After hanging up and grabbing her purse, placing her phone in it, she gave her dad another hug.

"Sorry Dad, I got to make a quick run. My friend needs me right now. After I'm done I will meet you back at your house."

"Okay. Sounds good. I'll be waiting along with DJ," Bishop replied before watching his daughter exit his office.

Chapter 25

Mocha paced back and forth in her kitchen awaiting the arrival of Erica.

Her anxiety was as high as a hooker's miniskirt from the info she possessed. Her spirit began overflowing with guilt, causing her neck and wrist to pulsate. She sat down and relit the high grade marijuana, inhaling deeply. As her nerves began to reach their natural state her stillness was interrupted by what sounded like someone trampling in her backyard area. As she cut off her kitchen light and peeked through the window nobody was in plain sight. She thought she saw a shadow but quickly dismissed it, blaming the marijuana. Her phone rang, startling her even more as she cut the kitchen light back on and walked to the kitchen table where her phone was previously placed. Glancing at the screen she noticed it was someone she was avoiding. Rejecting the call she placed the phone back down and went back to enjoying her smoking session. After placing the roach in the ashtray her phone began to ring once again. Mocha glanced at the screen then answered.

"What's up Dawud?"

"Nothing much. You tell me," Dawud said on the other end.

"Right now I'm chillin'. Just got finished enjoying a facial and now I'm waiting for my ace Erica to pull up."

"Wait, my baby mom Erica?"

"Yes what other Erica would I call my ace?"

"Look don't get smart. I only asked cause I thought she was supposed to be out Cali. Well at least that's what her Dad told me."

"She was out Cali. She came back for Deseree's funeral. And don't be trying to use me to fish for information about my girl."

Dawud started to chuckle before responding.

"Listen, I don't even get down like that. But speaking of Deseree that's why I was calling. I got interrogated for that incident and I was thinking ya boss and his sidekick had something to do with that."

"For real? That's crazy," Mocha said as her phone beeped, signaling another call was coming through.

After gazing she proceeded to answer her other line but not before dismissing Dawud.

"Look, that's E on the other line. I will call you back."

"Make sure you do 'cause I want to know what's up with them two," Dawud said before hanging up.

Mocha switched lines then spoke.

"What's up E? You out front?"

"Yeah girl, I'm out front."

"Okay, I will be out in a sec," Mocha responded.

The moment after she hung up she grabbed her keys, the last of her weed and Entourage, then placed them inside her purse. Taking a couple of steps towards the front door, she stopped in her tracks to ponder if she was forgetting anything. After coming to the conclusion she didn't she exited, walking a few feet then hopped in, joining Erica in her rented 300 C. Once inside they embraced as Mocha barked an order.

"Park real quick so I can roll up."

Erica placed the car in drive, maneuvered into the spot that was open on her right, then turned the car off, leaving the keys in the ignition. Erica turned to her right as she observed Mocha pulling out her accessories.

"Damn girl you smoking like it's 4/20. What's up?"

Mocha sighed heavily then replied.

"Girl you lucky you took that trip to Cali. Since you left it's been drama on top of drama. Speaking of Cali how did things turn out for you?"

Erica hesitated briefly then responded.

"Great. I got put on to this new opportunity and made some money."

Erica cleared her throat and swallowed her pride, leaving out the fact that she encountered some drama of her own. Mocha was her day one chick but she didn't feel comfortable yet with sharing the pertinent information that would cause her to look vulnerable. Mocha rolled the passenger window down, emptying the Entourage guts from the cigar then rolling the window back up. As she began licking the brown leaf she picked up where the conversation left off.

"That's what's up girl. Let me tell you since all this drama started I've been looking for a new way to make my money. I even looked into going back to school. Maybe this is a sign for me to change. You know what I'm saying?"

"I feel you Mocha. You got to do what's best for you. Now you keep bringing up drama. What's been going on since I left?"

A brief silence came between them as Mocha went into her purse grabbing her lighter and sparking it, drying up her saliva on the perfectly rolled vanilla Entourage. Once it dried she placed it in her mouth, sparked the other end, and inhaled.

"Well you already know about CC and Deseree. Soon after that Benji got busted by the Feds for running a continuous prostitution ring out of his clubs."

"Are you serious? Erica asked sincerely.

"Yeah, dead serious. Shit is crazy right now. That's why I'm trying to separate myself from the bullshit to get right for LeBron."

Erica nodded in agreement.

"You know what, great minds think alike 'cause I'm in transition myself. We ain't getting no younger. We got to make better decisions based on the future of our sons. Lord knows I don't want DJ to be in a position to make the same mistakes his dad made"

Mocha exhaled some smoke after taking a few puffs then addressed her best friend.

"Speaking of Dawud he called me before you pulled up."

Erica shook her head at Mocha mentioning her baby father.

"So what, he trying to fuck you too?"

Mocha scowled at Erica's reaction.

"Hell no! You know I wouldn't betray you like that. I value our friendship too much to even get down that way. He called to tell me he was taken in for questioning about what happened with Deseree and CC."

Erica's face eyes widened from the news.

"Oh my God. Are you serious? See I told him one day being community dick would catch up to him."

Mocha burst into laughter causing a choking reaction. After catching her composure she retorted.

"Girl you crazy. Community dick though."

Mocha wiped away a few tears that sprouted from the amusement then continued.

"You right though, but he called to discuss Benji and Omar 'cause he thought they were trying set him up or imply he had something to do with their deaths."

Erica shook her head as Mocha extended her right hand to pass her the L.

"Oh shit, my bad. I should've asked you first if you still smoke," Mocha stated as she pulled her arm back.

"You better pass me that weed bitch. When did I tell you I quit?"

Once in her possession Erica placed the tightly rolled wrap to her lips and took two long puffs. After forming a cloud of smoke inside the car she rolled down her window, letting the smoke out. While rolling the window back up she left a slight crack, taking two more puffs then glanced to her right in Mocha's direction. Erica instantly grew worried from the look that was plastered on her best friends face.

"No more weed for you. You over there looking like you need to 302'ed."

Mocha didn't even respond at Erica's observation as she remained staring frontward out of the windshield. A few seconds later she mustered up the courage to finally speak.

"Remember that Detective that helped you when you got caught up with that producer?"

Erica wrinkled her brow then replied.

"Yeah, why? What's up?"

"I need you to call her now. Tell her to meet us at Copa's on 40th and Spruce."

"Girl you wanna clue me in on why I'm calling her?" Erica asked as she started to get concerned.

Mocha put on the silent treatment again and just stared straight while Erica gazed at the left side of her face while taking a few more puffs. Parting her lips she exhaled and pulled out her cell phone, scrolling to Detective Richmond's number. Following the prompts she touched her screen as she began contacting her. On the third ring Detective Richmond answered.

"Detective Richmond. How can I assist you?"

"Yes Detective Richmond. This is Erica Williams."

"Oh hey girl. How's everything?"

"Okay I guess. Look, I have a friend that wanted me to contact you. Are you available?"

"Of course I'm available. Where should I meet you two?" Detective Richmond asked while pulling out her pen and pad.

"Right now we are on her block at 62nd and Catherine. She wants you to meet us at Copa's on 40th and Spruce."

"Okay, now what is this in reference to?"

"Hold on," Erica said as she peeped in Mocha's direction to communicate.

"Mocha she wants to know what the meeting is in reference to."

Mocha turned and replied with an eerie blank look.

"CC and Deseree."

Once she answered a car sped past, startling Erica as she was already breathless from Mocha's response.

"Hello," Detective Richmond uttered on the other end.

"I'm sorry Detective. This is in reference to CC and Deseree."

Detective Richmond hopped out of her desk seat then responded eagerly.

"Look, I will meet you two there in fifteen minutes."

Erica was in the process of pulling out of the parking space having to stop behind a tinted out black Buick Regal that needed a serious paint job. While trying to hold her phone by her right cheek and shoulder blade she released it from the slight clutch. Mocha reached down by her legs where the phone landed and picked up the phone. Erica, already impatient from the car just sitting in the same place, began to beep her horn before Mocha passed her the phone back.

"Hello Detective."

"Yes I'm still here," Detective Richmond answered on the other end.

"Look, I heard you. We are on our way as soon as I get around this jerk that's in front of us."

After Erica spoke a man hopped out of the vehicle brandishing a heavy metal instrument, aiming it in the direction of Erica and Mocha.

"Oh my God. Get down!" Mocha yelled out as she leaned over and pulled Erica down for cover.

Six shots were fired into the windshield as the assassin hopped back into his vehicle then sped off. Detective Richmond who was on the other end of the phone heard all six shots and responded rapidly, picking up her keys and transponder.

"Calling all available cruisers in the area. Shots fired on 62nd and Catherine. I repeat shots fired on 62nd and Catherine."

Chapter 26

Spanning from 63rd to 62nd and Catherine three patrol cars barricaded each end of the block while CSI was able to caution tape the scene. Six shell casings were circled and collected from the pavement and photographed. Residents in the vicinity sprawled the block with some questioning what transpired. Erica and Mocha were in the presence EMTs being treated for minor glass wounds. Detective Richmond decided to take a quick breather from questioning a couple of people to see if they had any visual of the incident. Before walking to her car she reported to one of the officers on the scene to come and get her once EMTs were finished with the victims.

"Officer Johnson I'm taking a quick R and R to make this important phone call to the Captain. Once the EMTs re done with the girls please come notify me."

"No problem Detective. I'm on it."

Detective Richmond sat in her car, reclined her seat halfway, and inhaled deeply. The case was starting to take a toll on her mental state and she couldn't wait to close it. Silently she prayed that this case would be solved from the info Mocha was about to present. As she withdrew from her conscious, Detective Richmond pulled out her cell phone and called Captain Morello.

"Tell me something good Detective," Captain Morello answered.

"At this point EMT has the victims Captain. I'm in my vehicle taking a breather from all of the chaos. But how I see it Captain the shooter knew the target had valuable information about this case and wanted to dispose of her."

Captain Morello exhaled as he contemplated.

"Okay, so based on that info get a patrol car to sit outside the victim's house for 24 hours until further notice."

"Perfect. I'll get officer Johnson for the job. Anything else I'm overlooking? I can't seem to think straight at the moment."

Captain Morello chuckled then responded.

"You're over-thinking the case again. Don't overwhelm yourself. This case will get solved. Just prepare yourself to be ready for whatever info the witness has for you."

"Okay Captain and thanks."

"No problem," Captain Morello replied as they hung up.

One minute later Detective Richmond noticed Officer Johnson approaching the car so she placed her seat upright and rolled down the window.

"Detective Richmond EMTs are finished with attending to the victims."

"Thanks Officer Johnson. Now onto orders from the Captain. Once everything clears up you have the honor of being the lookout for the overnight shift of the victim's house. You're to report any suspicious activity."

"Okay, I'm on it Detective."

Detective Richmond hopped out of her vehicle to attend to Mocha and Erica, who were walking in her direction both wrapped in red blankets.

"Detective could we speak in my house instead of going to the precinct?" Mocha asked.

"Of course. Whatever makes you comfortable," Detective Richmond obliged.

The scene started to clear up as residents began to step inside their row homes and patrol cars left. As instructed, Officer Johnson's remained and parked two spots away from Mocha's front door. Once inside Mocha walked straight into the kitchen along with Erica to partake in some tea and marijuana therapy.

"Detective you mind if we smoke while we talk?" Mocha asked.

"Once again at this point it's all about what makes you comfortable. We are in the comfort of your home. I'm here to collect the facts to close the case."

Mocha chuckled at Detective Richmond's response.

"Well I hope you got a lot of paper and ink 'cause I got a lot to share with you."

After speaking Mocha walked over to her sink and began to run water inside her teakettle, then placed it on the stove, turning on the front burner. Erica was sitting in silence while deconstructing the Entourage they were about to fill up with the finest hemp. Detective

Richmond's phone began to ring as she stepped out of the kitchen to take the call.

"What's up babe?"

"Nothing much. Over here holding onto Mandingo awaiting your arrival."

Detective Richmond was amused by Omar's nickname of his penis.

"Look, you and Mr. Mandingo got some more waiting to do. Something critical has taken place and it's related to my case. Once I'm done you and Mr. Mandingo can get all the time y'all want."

"Cool, go ahead and get back to work. Sorry for interrupting. Just know though when you get home you gon' get the business."

"Okay, can't wait," Detective Richmond responded as they hung up.

Detective Richmond reentered the kitchen, sat down, picked up her pen and pad, then glanced in Mocha's direction.

"Okay, it's time to get down business. What do you have to share with me when it comes to the deaths of CC and Deseree?"

Mocha took a deep breath and glanced over to Erica, who was as just as anxious as Detective Richmond to hear what news she possessed.

Chapter 27

Detective Richmond entered her house massaging the right side of her neck after an intense night of work. Upon arriving she was surprised by the candle lit entrance leading upstairs. A smile formed on her face as she took off her suit jacket then placed it the banister. Unbuttoning her blouse the slight change in temperature caused her nipples to poke through her black lace bra. As she began to make her way up the lit pathway two strong hands stopped her in her tracks.

"Where ya sexy ass going?" Omar asked as he fondled her breasts, bringing her back to his chest.

Detective Richmond grinned as she felt his manhood through her pants. She positioned her right arm behind her until she found the jackpot she was in search for.

"He's ready for you," Omar whispered in her ear.

Detective Richmond chuckled and wiggled her way out of his slight clutch, turning to face him.

"Let me get freshened up first then you and Mr. Mandingo can have y'all way."

Omar reached for her left wrist and pulled her so close where their eyes were centimeters away from each other.

"I want it now. Don't force me to take it," Omar stated forcefully.

Detective Richmond instantly became appalled about how Omar gripped her and tried to free herself but his kung fu grip overmatched her might.

"Omar you're starting to hurt me," Detective Richmond pleaded as she reached on the right side of her hip, forgetting she took her gun off her hip.

Omar tossed her to the wall as the impact knocked the wind out of her. Almost feeling like reality Detective Richmond awakened in the bath, causing a splash of water to hit the floor. A knock followed at the door, startling her even more as Omar announced his presence.

"What's taking you so long? You okay in there?"

Bath water trickled down Detective Richmond's body as she rose from the bath, grabbed her washcloth, and wiped her face before responding.

"Sorry babe, I fell asleep. I'll be out soon."

Detective Richmond treaded out of the bathtub, snatched out the water stopper, then wrapped her body in her towel fresh off the rack. Opening the bathroom door reminded her of the dream that just occurred as she noticed the candles leading out to her bedroom. As she opened the door Omar laid across her bed naked in the candle lit setting with a bottle of Moet and a bowl of chocolate covered strawberries.

"Champagne too? What are we celebrating?" Detective Richmond asked as she walked over to her dresser and pulled out a pair of black lace boy shorts, sat on the edge of her bed, and slid them on.

Omar ascended off his back and embraced her from behind. With his chest planted into her back Omar kissed her neck and placed both hands on her thighs, caressing them. Detective Richmond responded with a heavy moan as Omar spoke.

"Finally I can say I'm a boss and I don't have to answer to nobody. Everybody will have to take orders from me."

Detective Richmond spun out of his grasp and stood in front of Omar.

"What are you talking about?" she asked, frowning.

Omar, excited to share the news, explained without hesitation.

"I've been running around making sure that the clubs remain open. I paid off the fines and now all four will be back open while my former boss sits for those charges that almost took food out of my mouth."

Detective Richmond gleamed at the news.

"You're right, this is cause for a celebration. Now where's my glass Mr.?"

Omar stood and walked hastily over to where the bottle and glasses were and began pouring while Detective Richmond walked over to her dresser and went into her panty drawer, pulling out some handcuffs. Once Omar spotted the cuffs he paused in his tracks, instantly becoming inquisitive.

"What are they for?"

Detective Richmond beamed before responding while switching towards Omar.

"Just trying to bring some spontaneity into the situation and try something new. You not scared of little fun, are you?"

Holding both glasses Omar grinned from ear to ear while Detective Richmond seized one out of his right hand.

"Cheers to new beginnings," she mentioned before swallowing the liquid in one gulp.

Omar followed suit as he was overly excited about what was about to transpire. He took her glass along with the one he'd drank from and placed them on the side of the bed. Detective Richmond assumed control once he was done with the short task.

"Lay on your stomach," she instructed.

Without hesitation Omar plopped on his stomach as Detective Richmond slowly crawled on her bed. Starting at the bottom of his back she began giving him light pecks, working her way up to his neck. Once the kissing game was over she pulled out the cuffs, pulled his arms behind him, and placed the cuffs on his wrists. After stabilizing him she began kissing and sucking on his back again, leading up to his neck area. Once she made it to his ear lobes, she began whispering seductively.

"You're under arrest baby."

Omar wallowed under the spell of her voice as she began repeating her words in a normal tone.

"Omar you're under arrest for the murders of CC and Deseree. You have the right to remain silent. Anything you say can and will be used against you in a court of law."

Omar didn't budge. He just remained laying on his stomach with his head in the pillow still naked and handcuffed while Detective Richmond completed the Miranda then notified the precinct of the apprehension.

Chapter 28

"So what did I tell you? Sometimes you have to be patient with a case and let it come to you," Captain Morello said, speaking to his star detective.

He was excited about another big case being solved. He paused for a few seconds to gain his composure then began speaking again.

"Now despite the circumstances of who the culprit was I must say that was some savvy police work and I commend you Detective. You know I expected that to happen to your crazy partner over here, not you."

Detective Richmond glowed as she listened to the praise from her superior.

"You know what Captain, you're right," Detective Patterson reiterated. "That was some savvy police work. I even got the chance to hear one of the man's messages he sent while we were canvassing. I can only imagine how she felt when she found out she was sleeping with the enemy."

Detective Richmond shot her partner an evil glare after he used her for his own amusement. Captain Morello instantly put an end to Detective's Patterson shot at his 15 minutes of comedy fame.

"Give your partner a break. You don't see her busting your balls for your renegade work Downtown. Speaking of that, please don't let that happen again no matter what information you think someone is withholding. I received a few phone calls and they weren't from the Pope. So once again be mindful of your actions."

Detective Richmond switched her disposition once she heard about her partner's woes.

"Oh did Mr. GQ lose his cool?" she asked as she put her hand over her mouth sarcastically.

Detective Patterson chuckled at his partner then spoke on his transgressions.

"Captain I know I lost my cool but that guy was really being an asshole, excuse my French. I think even you would've pulled out your gun out on him. Everything he spoke on didn't add up and I got frustrated. Next time I will try and use better tactics to get information.

Captain Morello nodded then responded.

"Good to hear. Now as far as your case, we are at a standstill. All roads are leading to dead ends. I'm thinking that those bodies dropped were inside the faction and we witnessed it spread into the streets. Usually in this case everything will be quiet until money gets low and they are back into full swing of their operations. That's when we hit them with every combination we have.

Captain Morello sparked excitement within his detective.

"I say we go shake things up now to let them know we mean business; you know, run up in King's businesses to find out his whereabouts. Maybe even arrest some of his workers to see if we can pin that body, guns, and drugs on them."

Captain Morello shook his head then replied.

"You know they live by a code of silence. Plus they are trained to take the charges so the head still will be able to walk the streets. As far as the drugs that won't work 'cause you can't pin something on someone that doesn't exist at the moment."

Detective Patterson drew a blank from Captain Morello's last words as he pondered. Detective Richmond was curious as to why also since she was knee deep into her case. After thinking about it Detective Patterson responded.

"Sorry Captain but it slipped my mind that the evidence was never recovered. Were there any leads or follow ups based on that?"

Captain Morello hesitated as a knock came across his door.

"You may enter," Captain Morello announced as two suits that he was always familiar with walked inside.

As they entered Captain Morello rose up from his chair and played the perfect host to all those present.

"Officer Jennings, Officer Davis, these are my detectives Richmond and Patterson. I know you heard about Richmond's great work thwarting off a serial rapist/murderer."

"Yes, great work on your behalf Detective," Officer Jennings said shaking Detective Richmond's hand as Officer Davis stood by his side.

After the firm shake he continued.

"Now Captain Morello, on to why we are in your presence. We have intel that one of your officers is stealing evidence and selling it back on the streets. We have yet to receive a record of the last bust I believe Detective Patterson was involved in. Do you mind elaborating on that sir?"

Detective Patterson's palms instantly became sweaty as he started to answer. His voice began to crack as he cleared his throat then spoke.

"Yes I found—"

Detective Patterson was interrupted by Officer Davis' cell phone ringing and he stepped out of the office to answer. As he stepped out Officer Jennings addressed Detective Patterson while his partner and the captain sat in silence.

"We can pick up where we left off once my partner comes back in."

Detective Patterson nodded to Officer Jennings as Officer Davis treaded back into the office. He pulled Officer Jennings out of the office as they huddled together then thirty seconds later they reentered.

"Captain Morello that was my inside man. There's a deal going down tonight. Is there anything you or your detectives would like to share with us?"

Detectives Richmond and Patterson glanced at each other both puzzled as they sat silent while Captain Morello responded.

"These two are clear of any wrongdoings. As for myself, well my past speaks for itself, as you two already know. But I stand here before you to clear my name of any mishaps. Now as for the people that are guilty, that's another story so let's proceed with the investigation."

To be continued...

T. Real – Biography

Terrell Jones (Author T. Real) is a multifaceted person with credits under his belt that include author, playwright, graphic tee designer and entrepreneur. Born in Texas and being able to travel as a child, he found his own creativity through writing with influences from fiction greats like Donald Goines, Omar Tyree, Michael Baisden and Sistah Souljah. His vision proved to be outside the box and from life experiences a creative soul was born.

After signing his first publishing deal with Johnson Publications, Terrell went on to release his debut novel, *Homicide City*, and the later titles *Bitter Sweet* and *Cocktales*. Recognized for his writing ability he was also a contributing author for the reader's favorite anthology, *Erotic Snapshots* presented by Essence best-selling author, Anna J.

Wanting to have more control of his literary fate, Terrell launched his own publishing company, Made

Man Inc. and through this imprint he released *Cousin of Death* and upcoming works which include the sequel to his debut novel as well as the production of *Right Man Wrong Time,* a play based off of the novel of the same name and the release of his graphic tee line.

Currently, Terrell is a proud father who resides in Philadelphia who continues to create while leaving a legacy.

<u>Connect with T. Real</u>

Facebook.com/AuthorT.Real
Twitter: @trealdaauthor
Instagram: @trealdaauthor